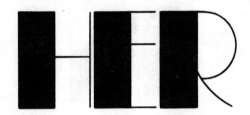

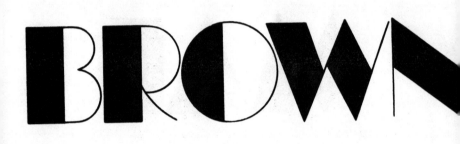

ISBN: 0-913780-14-6
Library of Congress Catalog Card Number: 76-7817

Published simultaneously in Canada by
Press Gang Publishers, Ltd., Vancouver, B.C.

Manufactured in the United States of America

**Second Printing**

Designed by Loretta Li

# DAUGHTERS, INC.

Plainfield, Vermont

ALSO BY RITA MAE BROWN

*The Hand that Cradles the Rock*
*Songs to a Handsome Woman*
*Rubyfruit Jungle*

FOR MYCHELLE SMILEY
The real Adele to my and the world's delight

# ACKNOWLEDGMENTS

I wish to thank Dolores Alexander and Jill Ward for allowing me to describe and use their restaurant, Mother Courage. I'm also grateful to Nina Finkelstein who took time out from her hectic schedule to give me good advice. Thanks to Rhoda Katerinsky for her encouragement and unfailing good humor. Ginger Ellsworth, Zoe Kamitses, and Lana Cantrell were friends above and beyond the call of duty to help type the manuscript. Linda Lachman put in a share of typing duty too. Special cheers to Jean O'Leary and again to Lana Cantrell for giving me the time to write the first draft. Barbara Boldtmann, Mary Molaghan, and Dr. Joanna Spiro were continual sources of hilarity. Matile and Harold Poor edited the first draft, a labor comparable to cleaning the Augean Stables. If any mess is left don't blame it on them but on the enormity of the task. Liz and Chris Poor and Elaine Noble provided diversion when I needed it most. Nancy Cunningham read the original manuscript and found Lester Maddox far too vulgar. Ever sensitive to criticism, when I reworked *In Her Day* I made him doubly foul. And praise be to Baby Jesus and Frip who perforated the manuscript with their teeth as well as walking over it lest I gain a reputation for neatness.

## NOTE TO THE FEMINIST READER

In art as in politics we must deal with people as they are not as we wish them to be. Only by working with the real can you get closer to the ideal.

## NOTE TO THE NONFEMINIST READER

What's wrong with you?

"Notice the sensuous curve of the breast."

The whirr of the slide projector didn't cover up the snicker of an immature male. Carole shot him a pitying look and continued with her lecture, "Ingres catches our eye with the sensation of movement and then holds us with a perfection of structure. As it's three we'll pick up where we left off next Tuesday. Let there be light, someone."

The room brightened and the robust women fondling each other in a Turkish harem faded from view. Carole gathered her notes then headed for the door. Three students quickly surrounded her for pearls of wisdom.

She nodded, "Have a good weekend," and raced for the elevator. Today wasn't the day for pearls. Crawling slowly down New York University's upper reaches, the elevator reminded Carole of mother possums, swaying under the weight of clutching children while backing down a tree. Possums and the Virginia summers of childhood receded from thought. A dangerous lurch on the fifth floor snapped Grandma's peeling house from memory and securely in the present Carole thought one of these days this damn thing will break and I'll plunge to my death with forty rich kids from Long Island.

The door opened onto the main floor spilling the human contents across the hall. Carole crossed Waverly Place to enter an even more decrepit elevator whose operator was in similar condition. Riley, his face a roadmap with all the lines drawn in fine purple, greeted her with an unfailing, "Top of the day to you, Professor Hanratty. Up to the art department, is it?"

"As always."

"Always watch the ball games in summer, you know." Since he was hard of hearing Riley answered with whatever he thought he heard. "You ever watch 'em?"

"Football not baseball."

"Baseball's an art. A real art. Nowadays everybody wants things fast. Me, I'm slow like this elevator. Love baseball, especially the Red Sox. Baseball and pinocle. Here we are."

"Thank you, Riley."

Directly across from the elevator loomed a spacious office, with wall-to-wall carpeting, and the large walnut desk curiously facing the elevator doors. Those doors opened and shut like the slide projectors which make up an art department's arsenal to attack uninterested post-adolescent minds. Resembling a student hypnotized by the changing images, Fred Fowler, head of the art department, blinked each time the doors revealed another passenger. It would have made sense to close the door or turn his desk around but Freddie Fowler didn't want to miss a thing, especially if the thing was female. The slight draft coming up the elevator shaft used to lift up their dresses but since the advent of pants barely a calf was to be seen. Still as the doors rattled, Freddie lifted his eyes and the gleam of hope burned there. Recognizing Carole's five foot eleven inch frame, slender and straight, the corner of his mouth twitched upward. "Carole, hello. How's the introductory course on such a hot day? The Great Neck heathens must be restless."

"Drugged is closer to the truth. Either the heat or downs depress them to a level of fuzzed attention although a few exhibit signs of active intelligence. In fact, Fred, I'm almost enjoying the summer session. Thought I'd hate it at first."

"Glad to hear that. Glad to hear that. I know how you feel. We gear ourselves to a semester cycle and want to race off for the summer."

"I'm racing off to check my mail. Have a good weekend, Chief."

"You too."

God, how Fred adores being called chief but then what can you expect of a man who hangs his coat-of-arms in his office? I swear he got his Ph. D. on the social significance of paint-by-numbers. And will he

5

ever raise his eyes above breast level? He says hello to my left tit. That guy will never give up. Carole reached into her mailbox and picked out the phone messages, backside up, spread them like a hand of bridge, closed her eyes and plucked one.

"Hi, Adele, just got back from class and got your message."

"Hey, darlin', what are you doing tonight?"

"Well, I was thinking of going to Rio de Janiero. On the other hand I might go to bed early."

"Uh-huh. LaVerne and I heard about a new restaurant in the Village, a kind of feminist eatery. Thought we'd try it. Want to join us?"

"Love to. What's the name of this place?"

"Mother Courage."

"My dear, do I have to wear an Equal Rights Amendment button to get in?"

"I doubt it. Just bring money. Sisterhood may be powerful but it's still poor."

"Okay. What time should I come over?"

"Seven-thirty? It'll take us a little while to get there."

"Seven-thirty's fine. See you then."

Adele hung up the black 1940's phone and stared into her garden.

I never thought I'd live to see thirty and here I am, forty-three. Carole's forty-four. I've known that woman for over twenty years. Close to a quarter of a century. Funny after all these years our friends are still trying to figure Carole out. She's easy enough for me to read. Must be her beauty. Americans make

6

icons out of beautiful women. Doesn't matter what a beauty does, she's misunderstood. Perhaps we're all misunderstood, they just get all the attention. Adele caught herself on that deflated thought and pushed her inner conversation with more vigor. Junior philosophers have been selling the essential loneliness of life since B.C. Nobody's understood and we're all alone in the cold, cruel world. I don't think people are lonely because they're misunderstood. They're lonely because they think they're misunderstood. Hell, they want to be misunderstood. That way they can be irresponsible. Besides, makes 'em think they're gifted or intelligent. Suffering in public is a genuine ambition. Ties in nicely with being misunderstood. Ha. Well, I understand Carole and she understands me. Maybe I know Carole better than I know LaVerne. Hell, I even know myself. I'm gonna put those limp philosophy departments out of business.

A piercing squack from Lester, a preening white cockatoo, shattered Adele's triumph.

"Shut up, Lester, you got no understanding. Furthermore, you got no couth, bird."

Lester unfurled his crown, let out another supersonic blast and relieved himself simultaneously.

"You are a filthy thing. You know that?"

If Lester knew he didn't let on. By now the two mackaws were gossiping loudly and the toucan, mynah, and plain green parrot became interested and were contributing to the conversation.

Adele, who could never be accused of being conventional, built an enormous bird cage all along one wall of her East 71st Street garden apartment. She told everyone it was little Africa although the style was Amazon rain forest. Carole dubbed it her jungle bunny wall. Adele spent far too much money on it with LaVerne bitching at every penny and calling her a spearchuker. The rock fountain, lush foliage, and brilliant, gabby birds were more than Verne could bear. Adele gloried in her creation. A woman has to have something of her own, lovers be damned. Carole sensed this and gave her Lester Maddox, a perfectly white cockatoo. Adele, in turn, taught Lester to say, "Bwana, White Devil!" everytime a non-Black entered her apartment. The first time Carole walked in and Lester laid his big line on her she nearly had a heart attack. Lester gave Adele more satisfaction than her Ph. D. in pre-Columbian art.

"Adele, where in hell is this place, in the river?" LaVerne sputtered.

"I forgot that the river doesn't run by Seventh Avenue," Adele apologized. "To tell you the truth I'm a bit lost. I never go below 57th Street. Speaking of going down, Carole, is Fred Fowler still after your ass?"

"He's incorrigible but about all he can do is leer."

"Honey, after all these years the poor man may be driven to such desperation he'll try rape," Adele hopefully noted.

"We'd have to charge him with assault with a dead weapon," Carole grinned.

Giggling they arrived in front of the little restaurant; the painted wooden sign creaked in the wind.

"Looks full. Imagine all these people trekking over here to the wild, wild West. Must be a good place," Verne commented.

They pushed the door open. People glanced up at them and then returned to their conversations and food.

A tall woman with a mobile face and a pleasant smile seated them at the lone unoccupied table.

LaVerne asked her, "How did they ever get this place together?"

"Are you all from out of town? Women in the movement from other cities usually ask that."

"No, we're from right here, the Hanging Gardens of Neon," Adele smiled.

"Oh. Well, I'm one of the people who started Mother Courage. It suddenly occurred to me one day over the frying pan that there were no restaurants for women. No place where we could gather and relax without being pushed or hunted by men. My friend knew a lot about business and I knew a lot about cooking and here we are."

The woman had such an engaging manner that by the time she finished her story all three women were focused on her, remarking how delightful everything was.

"I'm sorry I forgot to introduce myself. I'm Dolores Alexander."

Adele did the honors for the three of them.

"The kiev is very good and the broccoli moutard, if you're a vegetarian, has a delicious flavor. I hope you enjoy your evening with us."

A waitress walked by and Carole stopped her. "Excuse me, do you have coca cola?"

"No, but we have pepsi."

"No, thank you. We'll be ready to order in a minute if you'll come back to us."

"Think you'll last without a transfusion?" Adele ribbed her.

Carole threw her hand to her forehead, "Pepsi is vile, 7-Up insipid, and root beer quite out of the question. There. Wouldn't I have been wonderful on the Edwardian stage?"

"Or under it," LaVerne cooed.

"M-m-m. I recall a liquor store on Hudson. I'm going to run out and get two bottles of 'Southern champagne.' Adele, order me a spinach salad and the kiev."

She stood up and whirled around without looking. At that same moment a waitress who'd been in the kitchen all that time and who didn't know the table was filled charged around the corner with a tray full of salads. Carole glanced up just in time to see what was going to happen but not in time to get out of the way. The loaded tray hit her in the stomach, wobbled and clattered to the floor. Three salad bowls zipped toward the door and Carole's way was strewn with lettuce instead of palm branches. The dressing smelled wonderful. The waitress was mortified.

"Oh, I'm so sorry. It's all my fault. I didn't watch where I was going. Did I get any on you?" All in one embarrassed breath.

"We've got to stop meeting this way." Carole laughed to ease the waitress's discomfort.

The young woman blinked then laughed herself, "Are you sure you're all right?"

"I'm fine. How about you?"

"I'm okay. I think the floor caught most of it. Excuse me, I'd better clean this up before someone slips across the room.

Except for her apron the waitress looked as though she stepped out of an issue of *Mademoiselle* magazine. She was twenty-three at the most with sharp WASP features, blonde straight hair below her shoulders. She was white America's dream of femininity, a dream even Carole Hanratty couldn't quite purge from her loins.

In the late 1940's Carole was that dream when her own skin was so rich the oil shone on the surface, glowing as only the young can glow. Now she had evolved into a stately woman with a fine carriage and a noble, almost heroic head. Without ever being aware of it she eclipsed the simple radiance of youth.

The young waitress, thoroughly intimidated by the tall, self-possessed woman, fumbled the dust pan. There she was on her hands and knees dying a thousand deaths while this stunning, poised woman asked her again if she needed help. No, I need a quick and painless death she thought to herself. When Carole finally swept out the door in search of her coca cola the woman breathed a sigh of relief.

Adele, never one to miss a thing, chuckled.

When Carole returned with her two cokes in a little brown bag the spinach salad was on the table.

"Dell, are you sure you didn't scoop this up off the floor to torment me?"

"I want you to eat out of my hand not off the floor."

La Verne popped her fingers and swayed. She loved watching Adele and Carole together. A rare lover not to be jealous of such a close friendship, LaVerne appreciated their relationship. She was wise enough to

11

know that no one person fills another's needs. Carole gave Adele something she couldn't—a fast wit, refined literary tastes, and constant devilment. And LaVerne knew she gave exuberant, expansive Adele something Carole couldn't and that was a steadying hand lest all that energy fly off in a thousand directions at once.

"You know," Verne said, "the lights hanging over the tables look like the street lights we used to have when I was a kid in Trenton."

"Come to think of it they look like the street lights we had in Richmond," Carole replied.

"Ditto for St. Louis," Adele added. "Hell, maybe they really are street lights."

The collision waitress went by them and Adele called to her, "Ilse, are these old street lights?"

"Yeah, Jill Ward's got a hidden supply."

"Ilse James, allow me to re-introduce you to Carole Hanratty."

Carole leaned over and shook Ilse's hand. "I liked our original introduction, myself. Unforgettable."

"Really." Ilse used the word without realizing it belonged to a generation, hers. She hurried back to her duties.

"Well, Dolly Levi, how did you find out her name?" Carole's eyebrow arched over her right eye.

"Asked her. The three of us had a nice chat while she cleaned up the floor. That's the price of addiction to coca cola, my dear; you miss those intimate conversational moments."

"She is beautiful," LaVerne exclaimed.

"Beauty is in the eye of the beholder," Carole countered.

12

"Then you got big eyes," Adele teased.

"You two cupids attend to yourselves. When I was twenty-five I came to the depressing conclusion I'd never die from love although I did fling myself off a curbstone once when it became clear Katharine Hepburn would never marry me."

"Oh, stop." LaVerne's voice rose on stop.

"Verne's right. Stop stopping yourself. Love is the wild card of existence."

"No deal." Carole held on.

"Confess, you're a bit bewitched," Adele pressed.

"You two are starting to act like old maids. I thought matchmaking was how older women spun out their remaining years. Next thing I know you'll ask me for a finder's fee."

Adele and LaVerne laughed. Carole was trying to be morally indignant but the corner of her mouth twitched upward.

"Besides, since when is beauty the basis for love?"

"Now did you hear that come out of my mouth? All I said was, uh, Verne, what did I say?"

"Love is life's ace? Honey, don't do this to me. I haven't got total recall."

"And all these years I thought you hung on every word. Oh, I am so crushed." Adele stabbed a piece of broccoli and mournfully shoved it in her mouth. This posture lasted for all of two seconds. "I remember what I was saying. All I was saying was that people do notice each other physically."

"Right," the other two answered.

"Who knows when and whom we'll love but we try to find out first on the basis of physical attraction."

"I don't recall this philosophical note." Carole put

13

her head on her hand.

"Neither do I but it popped into my head."

"That and thirty-three other things simultaneous-ly." LaVerne squeezed Adele's knee.

"Actually, I've given this matter a little thought myself on those cold nights when I'm curled up in bed with the cats. A nasty strain of Puritanism lurks in most of us, I suspect. If there was one thing the Puritans couldn't stand it was a celebration of the body and beauty. So if we get attracted initially on the basis of looks we feel guilty about it or try to cover it up with the old business about 'she's beauti-ful inside and out.' "

"Wasn't it Mencken who said, 'Puritanism is the nagging suspicion that someone, somewhere, is having fun?' " Adele laughed.

"What a good quote. I'll pass that on to BonBon and Creampuff. Have either of you talked to them lately?" LaVerne asked.

"No, why?" Carole was puzzled.

"I spoke with Bon on the phone the other day. For some reason she was recalling the days of her stripper youth and she said when she first met Creampuff she noticed the curve of her neck. That's rather sexy. She also added that Creampuff had a sweet smile so she figured she was a lovely woman."

"I started this whole thing, didn't I?" Adele paused. "I wish to hell people would stop feeling guilty about everything and anything. I am so tired of people feeling guilty for sexuality or lack of it. I almost feel guilty for not feeling guilty!"

"Guilt is a Jewish invention improved upon by Christians for the last two thousand years," Carole mentioned.

Ilse nervously watched the three women as they ate their dessert and chattered among themselves. All the times she urged her friends to be aggressive were coming back to haunt her. She wanted to ask Carole out and if she didn't do it soon she might never see her again.

I can't walk up there and ask her in front of her friends, she thought to herself. I mean, what if she says no. Besides I can't put her on the spot like that. I wish she'd go to the bathroom then I could ask her on the way back. She probably has a bladder of cast iron. There's got to be some way to do this without making a total ass out of myself.

LaVerne got up to visit the can. Ilse figured one less observer was better than two so she gathered her courage, put her hands in her apron pockets so she couldn't wring them and walked over.

"Excuse me." Christ, all I say in front of this woman is *excuse me*.

They both looked up and Adele knew what was coming if Carole didn't. "I hope this isn't goodbye after we all just met."

Ilse stifled an impulse to hug Adele. "In fact, that's why I came over. I hope I get to see you again. I— uh—Carole, if you'd care to have a drink with me I think I could get off work early since the big rush is over. I . . . I mean if you're not in a hurry or anything." Ilse decided she had made a total ass out of herself. Maybe the kitchen would blow up and a flying pot would end this misery.

"I'd enjoy that. Why don't you go see if it's all right?"

"For sure!" Ilse, stunned by success, searched for

15

Dolores.

"Are you satisfied, you Cheshire cat?" Carole leaned over and pinched Adele's forefinger.

"Are you satisfied?" Adele couldn't help but laugh at her.

"You never let me get away with anything, do you? Yes, I'm satisfied. It's about time I let something happen. Anyway, after such a fateful meeting how could I refuse?"

LaVerne plopped down. "Some political soul inscribed on the wall, 'Peas with honor.' How perfect for a restaurant."

"Want to hear something else that's perfect? Ilse asked Carole to go out with her."

"No! That kid has guts."

"We both have to get up early tomorrow so how about if we go back home and you solo? You don't mind?" Adele asked Carole.

"No. I'll talk to you tomorrow and let you know how things turn out."

Settling in at the small table in a corner, Ilse looked at Carole then looked away. "May I ask you a question?"

My age, Carole thought.

"Are you in the women's movement?"

"What?" Carole's amazement showed.

"I mean are you in a group or do you read about it or anything?"

"That's the second time today the subject came up. Do I look like an Amazon?"

"No, you look intelligent," came the swift reply.

"Thank you. No, I'm not in any organization. I'm

not a very political person. Although I am glad some women are working for things that will benefit all of us, you know, like equal pay for equal work. But other than that I don't find that anyone represents my interests. I'm sure there's a great deal I don't know. I have only a surface understanding but as I said before, I'm not a very political person. I take it you are?"

"I'm in the movement, yes." Ilse smiled. "I can give you some together articles if you'll read them."

Suddenly Carole felt like a student but she didn't let her ego get in the way. "I'll read them."

"I'm a revolutionary feminist. I don't want you to think I'm one of those people who only wants a piece of the capitalist pie. We can build a whole new society, a cooperative society rather than a competitive one. That viewpoint is never represented in the pig media, you know?"

"I'm always afraid there will be enough revolutionaries to halt reform but not enough of you to make a revolution."

"I thought you said you weren't political?"

"I'm not but I do have eyes. Anyway, in America the word revolutionary is used to sell pantyhose."

Ilse laughed in spite of herself. Was Carole witty or making fun of her? Ilse spent the last two years of her life "in struggle" and while she learned a lot she lost more: her sense of humor. Carole's obvious irreverence awakened that sense of humor and it seemed heady, even dangerous. She stared at the older woman and tried to come to grips with her physical presence.

The first thing anyone noticed about Carole was

her height. She was six feet tall depending on the day. Once people recovered from that they observed her head. Thick, brown, medium length hair was brushed back revealing heavy silver over each temple. The silver was offset by small gold earrings. Her nose was long, straight, with delicate nostrils. Her forehead was high. Very English, thought Ilse, or perhaps high Irish. Her cheekbones were sharp and prominent, the jaw firm, the mouth sensuous, full. Deep creases surrounded her mouth and her eyes showed marked laugh lines. She exuded a self-confidence that, together with her physical being, made her compelling.

"Would you like to dance?" Ilse decided to table the political discussion.

"If we decide who leads before we get out there?"

"You, you're taller."

As it was a weeknight the women's bar was only half full when they arrived and there was room on the dance floor. Carole hadn't danced in a long time and the body contact hit her. She hadn't done anything in a long time. Ilse rested one arm around her neck and the other around her waist drawing them tightly together. Temples throbbing, Carole couldn't look down at the younger woman or she knew she'd kiss her. The irony of the situation didn't escape her. She'd never kissed a woman in a bar in her life, much less the first time she met someone.

Ilse didn't look up or try to converse until the song started to fade. Then she turned her face up, the faint light revealing eyes of such a light, pure hazel they were practically clear. Without one more word of internal monologue Carole bent over and kissed her. It was one of the few times in her life since age twelve that she acted like a true animal. The freedom was intoxicating.

"My god, what would Emily Post think?" she said.

"Emily'd think you were one hell of a kisser." Ilse tossed her hair out of the way, put both hands on Carole's face and returned the kiss. Barry White boomed in the background and they danced one more.

"Will you go to bed with me?"

Carole was shocked. No one, woman or man, ever said such a thing in so short a time. It took months for people to get around to that question and no one dared ask it directly. They tried to sneak up on you usually on the path of a common interest.

No charades before the procession into the bedroom, this is a new generation, she thought.

Ilse, seeing her hesitate, quickly added, "I didn't mean to make you uptight. I thought it would be a beautiful thing to do. I don't want you to feel hassled."

"I admit I'm not used to such a direct and fast approach but you can ask me that anytime you like. However, tonight's not a good night because I have to get up early tomorrow."

"Tomorrow night?"

Carole decided not to think, "All right."

"If you want to pick me up at work that's okay, or I could meet you somewhere. Oh wait, I forgot, a singer is coming into the restaurant tomorrow night so I have to stay until she's done. You might dig her."

"It isn't that electric screeching, is it?"

"No. The woman uses a regular guitar."

"What time does she go on?"

19

"Around ten."

"I'll see you tomorrow at ten." She stood up to leave.

"Right, unless the revolution starts tomorrow I'll be there."

"Ilse, I think the revolution already started." Carole smiled and kissed her goodnight.


Adele called Carole after her first class the next day. "Well?"

"Well what, you relentless old gossip?"

"I'm parched for news. What happened last night?"

"We talked and danced a bit."

"And?"

"And I came home alone because I had to teach this morning. Honest to god, Adele, I thought we left these conversations back in our twenties."

"Harrumph. BonBon, Creampuff, and I have them all the time, my dear. Anyway, Verne and I made a bet and I lost, dammit."

"You're terrible."

"No, I'm not. What's so bad about putting a few coins on the optimism of the flesh? Besides, people don't court anymore so I thought maybe that young lady just pulled you right into bed, honey."

"She did ask."

"Maybe I can win half the bet."

"That'll be a first. Not with LaVerne you won't."

"Ain't that the beautiful truth! That woman pinches a nickel until the Indian rides the buffalo."

"I'd be willing to bet people are more emotional about money than they are about sex."

"Amen. They tell you more about themselves when

they spend a dollar than when they spend the night with you."

"Which reminds me, you might be able to recoup some of your losses if you bet on tonight."

"Carole, you amaze me."

"Darlin', I amaze myself."

"When in Rome, etc."

"Something like that. Since I've never done anything like this, at least not in such a short time span, I figured I ought to try it. Aren't you the one who always says, 'Progress lies in the direction you haven't been?'"

"Yes, but I never said the direction was horizontal."

"You devil, talk to you later. Give Verne a kiss and damn don't you be telling BonBon Yvonne and Creampuff Louise what I'm about. Those two will have it all over town."

"I told Bon yesterday that with all the information she has, she could get rich overnight."

"Blackmail?"

"Hell no, she can start a special service for lonely women, Dial-a-Dyke."

"Mary, Mother of God." Carole howled.

"She can use it too. Bon and Creampuff aren't prejudiced."

"Adele, you are one of a kind. Now I am hanging up this phone or I won't be able to get a thing done the rest of the day. Bye, love."

Carole showed up around ten-twenty but Ilse was convinced fifteen minutes after ten that she'd never see her again. When Carole did walk in, the place was so packed Ilse couldn't get over to her so she waved and tried to not look too excited.

Listening to the singer, Maxine Feldman, Carole surveyed the room. The crowd with few exceptions was under thirty and downwardly mobile. It was wall-to-wall workshirts with embroidery to relieve the monotonous blue. Little, enameled, five-pointed, purple stars stood out on caps and shirts. Carole noticed Ilse wore one on her left sleeve, over her bicep. Maxine displayed one on the bib of her overalls. They were pretty but Carole had no idea what they meant.

So many of these people tried to look unattractive and that disturbed Carole. A few of them even looked dirty. Poor as she and her family were in the Depression, they were always clean. If her mother came back from the grave and saw some of these people it'd kill her all over again. Perhaps it wasn't that the women tried to look ugly. Maybe they just didn't care. Carole checked them out again.

A few look like you could plant seeds on them, she noted, but the group isn't all that bad. Maybe it's a fad like bobby sox and Dad's shirt was in the forties. And saddle shoes. I remember I had a pair with black saddles and then brown ones came in. Gawd. Still these people do look in uniform. I guess we did too but you can't see yourself at that age. I wonder if wearing a purple star and patched pants is like being a Franciscan and taking a vow of poverty?

Women in the room cheered the singer—"more, more"—after she finished a driving song about Marilyn Monroe. Carole wasn't much interested in Marilyn when she was alive much less dead. But a chill swept down her spine. The lyrics reached her. Color rose to her face when she realized she had made some tenuous connection with woman as a group. She hadn't realized that, until now, she had believed there were men, women, and herself.

No, she thought, not quite that cut and dried. I guess I've always thought there was an intellectual elite and people like myself and Adele are part of it. Brains transcend genitals.

Ilse made her way through the crowd as Maxine took a much deserved break.

"Do you have anything left to do here?" Carole asked.

"No, let's go. My apartment is on 12th Street. We can walk over there, it's not far. It's easier to talk there than here or at the bar."

Underneath the West Side Highway, moonlight flickered on the old Erie-Lackawana buildings on the other side. A heavy river smell rose up in the July night.

"It's another world down here. Haunted."

"Wait until you see the building my apartment is in. I think it was built in the early nineteenth century. A sea captain built it for his mistresses and I live in the tiny cottage in the courtyard where he kept the number one lady."

The door to the stucco, crumbling apartment building, not but two stories high, was a bright blue. It opened into a long hallway and at the end of the hallway was another blue door, possibly bright but who could tell in the dim light. Ilse reached into her jeans pocket, pulled out keys on a long chain that was hooked to her belt loop, and unlocked the door.

"Isn't this a trip?"

"It's charming. The courtyard looks like something out of Vermeer."

French windows were opened to catch what cool breeze there was and patches of small flowers, closed for the night, hinted that the days were colorful. Flat stones paved the enclosure and a high wall refused entrance to the rest of New York City.

"Each set of windows is an apartment," Ilse said in a low voice. "There are two wings and the middle apartments in the wings have little balconies. You should see the narrow, winding staircases those people climb. But the balconies are very romantic. A friend lives in the left one over there and she puts up flags so signal me."

"Do you signal back?"

"Yeah, I hang mine out my side window, see," she pointed around the small cottage and there a red and yellow pennant fluttered sporadically. "That's my great day flag. My flowers are coming along and over there's a bird feeder. Come on, let's go inside."

She opened the door into a small room where two cinder blocks under each side of a piece of plywood served as a low desk, a cushion for a chair. A few handfuls of books surrounded the desk. Off to the left was a slightly larger room with a bed against the wall, covered with an Indian print. Over the bed was a poster of multicolored little women in circle after circle holding hands. A fireplace was six feet from the bed. The walls were startling, bone-white stucco. On the other side of her desk was the bathroom, and the kitchen was a miniscule refrigerator and stove not ten feet opposite the fireplace. A dilapidated make-up dresser was right by the door.

24

"This is out of another century. All you need is a thatched roof," Carole exclaimed.

"I know. I dig it. In the winter the fireplace is the only heat I have but the place is so small it keeps me warm. The only trouble is keeping the wood dry outside so I always have to be sure to have fifteen logs stacked up by the frigie or it's blue lips Ilse."

"Is that the bathroom over there?"

"If you want to take a shower, call me and I'll join you."

"Took one before I went out," Carole answered, closing the door. When she came out she noticed Ilse had turned off her one overhead light and now a fat candle glowed in a low dish. Next to it in a Lancer's bottle were lavender and blue straw flowers.

"You can take one with me or wait, I won't be long. Running around serving all night, in and out of that steaming kitchen, makes me a prime candidate for Dial soap."

"I'll wait."

As there was no place to sit other than the floor, Carole crawled over on the bed and leaned out the French windows. The courtyard, silver in the moonlight, was noiseless. A fat cat looked down at Carole from her perch on the left balcony. Not far away a deep call came from the river, a tug pulling its prize in from the sea. The shower drizzle stopped and Ilse, wrapped in a terrycloth robe, emerged from the bathroom. As she offered Carole tea it struck her that she had talked politics last night and forgot to ask Carole what she did, so she asked.

"I'm a professor of art history at New York University. My field is medieval art and I'll stop there or

I won't stop until I've outlined the whole thirteenth century."

"When I was at Vassar I had a fantastic art history professor. I always thought that stuff was dull and dry until she taught me that ideas could be transmitted visually. That was such a revelation to me. I was so bound to the word, you know what I mean?"

"When were you at Vassar?"

"I graduated in 1973."

"I graduated in 1951."

"Oh, wow."

"However, when I was at Vassar there wasn't a women's movement except in the direction of Yale."

"I can dig that," Ilse muttered.

"I couldn't. All those silly girls fluttering around a Skull and Bones man."

Ilse frowned. "Know what you mean. It is pretty disgusting when women act giddy and dumb around men but in 1951 what kind of choices were there? I mean, we need to recognize people in their oppressed places. Like oppressed in their heads because Vassar isn't for poor women. But rich or poor, women are brought up to be half-people. There really wasn't an alternative to the Skull and Bones man."

"You're looking at the alternative." Carole smiled but Ilse picked up the sternness in her voice.

What an unusual woman, Ilse kept thinking. She's a proto-feminist, a rebel who doesn't know it.

It never once occurred to Ilse that she was telling Carole about 1951 and the behavior of women when Carole was right there and Ilse wasn't even walking yet. Carole's partly opened blouse gave a glimpse of full breasts. Tempted by the sight Ilse forgot to

26

launch into her riff about women's identity. She ran her forefinger from the hollow of Carole's neck down to the middle of her stomach, unbuttoning with her left hand as she went along. The older woman shivered, leaned over and without the slightest pressure gently kissed her, kissed her neck, the line of her jaw and her lips once more, harder this time.

Ilse pulled down the covers and threw her robe off. "Should I start a drum roll?"

"That's funny because I have two friends who are ex-strippers. I've often wondered if they played that music when they went to bed," Carole remarked, slipping her arms out of the silk blouse.

Her shoulders were broad, her hips slim and tight; Ilse reached out and pulled her into bed without ceremony. She put her arms around her neck and pushed her somewhat smaller frame into the long body. All that cool flesh made Ilse shudder. Carole bit her neck while dragging her fingernails all along Ilse's side. Goosebumps covered both of them making them laugh in the middle of a kiss. Carole pushed Ilse's blonde hair out of the way, kissing her forehead, cheeks, nose, and lips. She parted the young woman's teeth with a dart of the tongue. Ilse moaned and held onto Carole with such force she left fingerprints all over her back. Pressing the small of the young woman's back Carole welded them together, the sweat sliding from their torsos onto the bed. Carole felt Ilse's fingers on the back of her neck threading up through her hair and she put her forehead between the younger woman's small breasts. Ilse arched her back and brought her legs up around Carole's waist. Carole could feel the muscles running along the inside

27

of the thighs. Each woman marveled at the shape of the other, the white of their teeth flashing with their smiles and sounds. Ilse lifted Carole up off her body with strong tanned legs and rolled her over on her side. Her hand lay on Carole's flank. The idea of that hand proved inflammatory. Carole reached over caressing Ilse's upper thigh. They couldn't stay there for long; the tension, the sweat, and the searching lips demanded resolution.

"Carole?"

"H-m-m?"

"You're driving me crazy. I don't know your body yet, I don't know what you want."

"What do you want?"

"I want to make you come," Ilse whispered in her ear.

"Don't worry. We'll get there soon enough," Carole whispered, slowly traveling up her thigh to push inside her. Ilse strained against the long fingers, pointing her toes, carrying the sensation through her entire body. As Carole moved away Ilse reached down and caught her and the two women hung suspended in mutual pleasure but not knowing one another well enough to pull it off.

"We can come back to me," Carole breathed.

"Sure?"

"Sure."

Ilse wasn't certain what was going on. She could feel Carole touching her with both hands as they lay side by side, kissing her neck, filling her mouth with her tongue. All she could think was she's so slow and she's so sexy and then she stopped thinking, the rest of her body silencing her ever-talkative cerebrum.

28

Carole leaned up on one elbow cupping her head with her left hand, and with her right hand she stroked the hair off Ilse's wet forehead. Ilse, too limp to move, started laughing and turned her face to Carole whose eyebrows asked why.

"It's so good. I mean if we can do this first time out!" Ilse exclaimed.

"Practice makes perfect."

"Carole, I knew you were going to say that."

"It was a set up."

"What can I do for you?"

"When you catch your breath lie on top of me. We can get acrobatic later at another practice session."

"Got my breath back." Ilse landed on her with a war whoop.

"My god, I'm in bed with Sheena Queen of the Jungle?" Carole pulled her hands down from Ilse's neck to her tiny bottom and moved her own body against the smooth skin. Carole could feel the muscles tightening and relaxing across both of their flat stomachs. The heat, the motion, the shiny hair washing against her face brought Carole to a series of upheavals that astonished Ilse. Carole lifted her off and blew against Ilse's skin to cool it.

"You really are incredible," Ilse gasped.

"No, I've just been practicing longer than you. Sex gets easier and better as you get older."

"Not for men it doesn't."

"Well," Carole grinned. "I'm speaking for myself. Men will have to speak for themselves on that subject."

"Don't let me forget in the morning to ask you a favor."

"Ask me now so I can prepare for it," Carole answered as they snuggled under the sheets.

"It's not such a big one. Will you help me carry that old make-up dresser out to the sidewalk? It isn't heavy but it's too awkward for one person to carry. It was here when I moved in and it's driving me bonkers."

"M-m-m, kiss me first."

Ilse kissed her lips, played with the corner of her mouth, and then outlined Carole's mouth as slowly as if she were a snail on her appointed rounds.

"I'll do it." Carole laughed at herself.

As Carole opened her eyes she saw, staring down at her, two glittering, green ones. A large tabby lounged in the windowsill, her stiff whiskers coming forward like a bowtie when Carole sat up. Ilse was still asleep so Carole gingerly moved over her, only to have the cat pounce square in the middle of Ilse's back.

"What!" Ilse pushed up and blinked.

"Either that's your cat or you have a bold visitor."

"Here, Vito." The cat jumped up to Ilse's face and rubbed a furry forehead on Ilse's own forehead. "Vito Russo's my cat but at night when she prowls she climbs up the vine and stays with Lucia. So she's half Lucia's. What time is it?"

"Ten-thirty. Damn, I slept with my watch on."

"Time to get up. After I feed Tootsie, I'll feed you."

"All I need is tea to get me going and an English muffin if you have one."

"You're in luck."

After breakfast Carole informed Ilse she had to get back home soon because she wanted to work on a paper she was preparing for publication.

"What kind of paper?"

"Art history stuff."

"Oh. Well, will you help me move out that make-up dresser before you go?"

"A promise is a promise," replied Carole.

Ilse picked up one end of it. "See, it isn't heavy at all but it's too big for me to get my arms around it."

"The flowered material hanging all around it is enough to blind people. Are you sure you should put it on the street?"

Ilse threw up her hands. "What do you mean? That's why I want to put it on the street. You think I want to look at it? Besides, I don't wear make-up so it's sitting here like dinosaur bones."

The only difficulty they had getting the visual horror out to the street was in the narrow hallway in the main apartment building, but with a few scraped knuckles they succeeded in setting it firmly on the sidewalk.

"Hey, did you ever watch 'Candid Camera?' " Ilse questioned.

"Once or twice, why? That was ten or fifteen years ago."

"I was pretty little when it was first around but I remember they used to do hysterical things like rig a talking mailbox or stop catsup bottles so they would-n't flow and people would freak out, you know?"

Carole's eyebrows raised but she remained silent. Was this a *non sequitur* or was Ilse leading up to something?

"Carole?"

"What?"

"Let's get under this thing and stick our heads out when people come to scavenge it. The material reaches to the ground; they'll never know we're under there."

"I will not. Put anything on a New York City sidewalk and five people descend instantly to fight over it. We might sustain serious injuries."

"That's not the real reason. You're uptight. Come on, no one is going to know there's a respectable professor lurking under there."

"That's right. No one would believe it. They'll think I escaped from Bellevue."

"Please," Ilse pleaded. "It'd be fun. And what do we care? We'll never see any of these people again. This is New York, remember?" She tugged at Carole's sleeve and looked up at her the way a dog does when it wants a table scrap.

"What the hell." Politely lifting the edge of the cloth as though it were a skirt, Carole motioned for Ilse to precede her. Ilse scurried under. Carole hesitated.

"Come on." Ilse stuck out her head.

Carole dropped to her hands and knees and crawled under. "Tight fit."

"Yeah," agreed Ilse, "but if you stay on your haunches you can stick your head up under the empty drawer. I think the empty drawer is on your side."

"It's here."

"Good, you'll have more room. You're a lot taller than I am. You okay?"

"I'm okay."

"Me too, I'm fine down here. I feel like a tarantula waiting to spring at my prey."

"If you keep jabbering you won't lure anything," Carole reminded her.

"Oh, right." Ilse shut up and not five minutes later a light footfall approached the dresser. A hand could be heard smoothing over the top. Ilse elbowed Carole since Carole couldn't see anything other than the garish print.

"S-s-st, move to the left," Ilse breathed.

They took two tiny steps to the left. The feet in front of them jumped back. Ilse let out a jubilant laugh and stuck her head out to find another woman, closer to her own age, resplendent in patched pants.

"Fooled you,"

"Far out. Wow, are you stoned? I mean totaled?"

"No," Ilse replied. "We're just goofing."

"That's so far out." The woman babbled, wandering off in the direction of Hudson Street.

"Was she blasted, qualludes," Ilse reported. "I hate to see sisters on any kind of shit. There is so much shit circulating in this city, I swear the Feds are hawking it."

"It's either or," Carole piped up.

"Huh?"

"My generation is juiced and yours kills itself on narcotics. I wish people would kill themselves quick and get it over with. I don't see why I have to be imposed on by people destroying themselves and calling it sociable."

"You have to realize people do it to dull the pain."

"Bullshit." Carole changed the subject. "I can't see anything with my head stuck up in here. Let's get out, we had our fun."

"Oh, a few minutes more, okay?"

"Grumble," was the reply. "Ouch!" Ilse pinched her ass.

Heavy footsteps thundered in their direction. It felt like a two ton truck was barreling right for them. A mutt stuck its head under the make-up dresser. The dog was too surprised to bark. Tips of Murray's Space shoes showed under the fabric, nearly touching Carole's shoes. Ilse, inspired, leaned forward and seized the person by the ankles. A groan followed by a terrible thud worried Carole. "What's going on out there?" Sticking her head out like a wary turtle Ilse gasped, "Christ, he's fainted and he's near to three hundred pounds! Bet he cracked his skull and died. Let's split." She wiggled onto the sidewalk and started walking away thinking Carole was right behind her. She turned around to discover she was alone in her escape. Running back to the dresser she picked up the fabric and beheld Carole's head framed by the square space for the dresser drawer.

"You look like Senor Wensclas," she said. "Need help?"

"I'm stuck, goddammit."

"This is no time to get stuck. We'd better get out of here before that hippopotamus comes to. We'd probably be better off if he had cracked his skull and died than if he finds us."

A man walking with his afghan far down the street pranced in their direction and there was someone else behind him.

"Ilse, I'm stuck, I tell you."

"That's impossible. Professors don't get stuck under dressers in broad daylight on the streets of New York."

"This professor is wedged in at the shoulders and can't get out of here."

"Well—then start moving. We've got to vanish before this guy lays eyes on us and all of Greenwich Village shows up."

"You're crazy. How can I walk in this thing?"

"Do you want him to look under there and find you by yourself because I'm not sticking around here. Start walking."

"Don't you at least think you ought to take a closer look at him to see if he's okay?"

Ilse tiptoed over and peered at the victim, then tiptoed back. "He's out cold. The guy is so round he couldn't really fall down hard and hurt himself."

A sigh struggled out of the top drawer and the fabric swayed out with it. Carole mumbled, "You walk beside me and guide me. I feel like a blind crab."

"Okay, okay, keep moving to the left. We're going up 12th now. Faster, Carole, faster, we have to get around the corner. I see him stirring." The empty drawers rattled as Carole picked up speed.

"Okay, now turn halfway around and start moving towards the right, then he can't see us."

"Are we out of range yet?"

"Yeah, now let me look at you again."

"Pull the cloth back and you can see me better."

"Say Sallright."

"S'not sallright. Now stop laughing and get me out of this thing."

Ilse got down on her hands and knees for a better view. "Damn, you are really wedged in there. Try lying on your back and maybe I can worm you out."

"I can't lie on my back."

"Yes, you can. Sit down and then fall back. I'll catch you. Careful, careful. There you go."

Carole's legs twitched up in the air. "I'm half suspended in this thing and the wood is cutting into my back. Lift up, come on, this hurts."

"Well, then we'll have to go a little farther down the street to the deli. Castellani's bound to have a hammer or something I can use to knock you out or pry you out."

"How far is the deli?"

"A block or so."

"For the love of god."

The two made their way down the street. A few passersby gaped but most looked straight ahead as though: if you've seen one walking dresser, you've seen them all.

"Hold it, Carole. We're at a corner. Let me scout in case that guy is hunting for us."

"Hunting for us? He probably woke up, thought he hallucinated, and sped for home as fast as possible."

"The coast is clear. Watch out now. Can you look down and see the curb?"

"No! All I can see is this hideous fabric. That's even worse than getting stuck under here."

"Okay, now step down. Try to gas it up so we can get across the street. Stop. Okay. Up you go."

"Shit, this thing is getting heavier than when I started out."

"Just a little further, Carole. You know what Mao says."

"What the hell has Mao got to do with getting stuck under a make-up dresser? Next you're going to tell me he's a drag queen."

"Perseverance furthers," Ilse answered.

"That's hardly an original thought. Do Mao a favor and don't hang that one on the good chairman." Carole was tiring. The drawers were quieter now as she shuffled down the pavement.

"Stop. We're here. You stay outside while I go and see if Mr. Castellani has any tools."

"Where could I possibly go in this old thing?"

"The Museum of Modern Art?" Ilse tried.

"Boo. Hiss. Hurry up will you."

Carole squatted, collecting her breath.

Bam! She was shaken. Wham! Another violent shake. Slowly she was being dragged down the street. She dug her heels to put on the brakes. That did no good.

"This sonofobitch is heavy. I thought these things was supposed to be light?"

"Yeah, maybe there's stuff in the drawers."

Carole yelled, "Let me go!"

"John, you hear somethin'?"

In her best and loudest Miss Marple, Carole bellowed, "Unhand me!" The dresser came down with a thud.

"What the fuck?" A hairy hand pulled back the fabric to see Carole's angry face glaring back at him. "Lady, you're nuts!"

"You're telling me. Now go away and leave me in peace. It's not safe any more for a woman to walk the streets alone."

Ilse emerged from the deli just in time to see two large men clad in shirts with Wonderbread emblazoned across the back in script stomping off shaking their heads and gesturing.

"Carole, are you all right?"

"Ilse. Men have tried to pick me up before but this time they did it literally. Now will you please get me out of here!"

"This might hurt a little."

"That's secondary to the embarrassment."

Ilse on her back paddled under the dresser and started knocking the front leg off.

"Wouldn't it be easier to do it from the outside?" Carole asked.

"Yeah, but if the leg splinters, then it splinters in at you."

"Oh."

Two solid blows and the leg squeaked out of place.

"Let me get the back leg and then I think I can get you out." Ilse pounded the back leg as Carol winced.

"It's coming, come on, baby, give," Ilse grunted.

"Don't talk dirty, dear, just get me out."

"Well, don't make me laugh or I'll get weak and it'll take that much longer."

A choking laugh floated out through the empty drawer. Ilse pounded the back leg until it collapsed and the whole dresser sagged on both of them. She held the top half of the dresser with her right hand and pushed her left foot up against the drawer space which had been partly splintered.

"Got it. Got it. Squeeze out."

Carole rubbed her shoulder and quipped, "I'm a liberated woman."

"Oh Carole, I'm sorry." Ilse massaged her shoulder, rubbed the back of her neck. "I really am sorry." But she couldn't keep from laughing. "I am sorry but you looked so funny and if you could have only seen that fat dude!" Ilse, bent over with laughter, sat down next to the rubble dropping Mr. Castellani's hammer.

Carole, her legs aching, staggered a few steps and folded next to her on the sidewalk.

"You're a good sport." Ilse threw her arms around her.

Carole glanced at her sideways and broke up. Ilse was laughing so hard the tears came to her eyes. "Come here." She pulled Carole to her and gave her a kiss.

When was the last time I laughed this hard? Carole wondered. When was the last time something unexpected happened or that I let something unexpected happen? I've lost my sense of play. When I laugh it's over words. Wit. Intellect. I remember—I remember when I was a kid we'd get into scrapes like this. Where did that go? When did it leave me? I want it back. I want it all back.

A crash and loud curse made them jump apart. A man riding a bicycle wrapped himself around a No Parking sign. Groceries were all over the street but he was so mortified he wouldn't even look at the cause of his crash and pedaled on with his rear wheel out of line, leaving his debris behind him.

"What next," Carole exclaimed and they fell all over themselves.

Ilse wiped her nose and eyes, helped Carole up, then took the hammer back to Mr. Castellani. She brushed off Carole's backside. "Are you all right now?"

"That isn't where it hurts. I'm okay. Listen, I have to get home to work on that paper."

"Okay. I ought to go over to the workspace and

help collate some stuff."

"Workspace?"

"Yeah, a bunch of women have a loft floor over on Waverly and Mercer, right by N.Y.U. in fact, and we all pay a low rent and have a place to work."

"What a good idea."

"Will I ever see you again? I seem to make one mistake after another."

"Come up tonight after work if you like. You can rub my shoulders."

Ilse, relieved and happy, asked, "Where do you live?"

"114 East 73rd between Park and Lex. It's a brownstone and I'm on the top floor. Ring the bell."

"Terrific, I'll be there."

Carole added, "I know, unless the revolution starts today."


When the tiny elevator stopped at the ninth floor the door into the workspace was locked. Ilse pulled her keys on the long chain out of her pocket and unlocked it while the elevator door banged into her rhythmically. As she opened the door a small knot of women looked up and greeted her. Piles of papers lay in neat stacks and people sat on the floor in a miniature assembly line putting the pamphlets together. Ilse volunteered to be an additional stapler and soon she was crunching away.

Olive Holloway started in on her. "Who was that we saw you with last night, your mother?"

Alice Reardon, who couldn't stand Olive, cut her off. "Shove it, Holloway. We don't need that ageist crap around here."

40

Olive, usually able to guilt trip her way out of anything, was stuck for once and went back to her chores. Skilled in emotional blackmail, Olive constantly gummed up meetings with her Esalen techniques. If that failed she could always cry since her eyes were connected to her bladder. She'd sob, "You all are oppressing me." Most of the women in the group by this time cordially detested her but no one was quite sure how to get rid of her. It didn't seem sisterly to bounce her so they sacrificed the welfare of their group instead. Ilse was beginning to realize that their inability to eject someone who was a thorn in their side was part and parcel of white middle-class women's conditioning. Be nice. It was burnt into their brains at an early age. And here they all were being nice to a viper. For a time Ilse thought maybe Olive was an agent. Her friends in the peace movement supplied her with the characteristics of every conceivable type of agent: the provacateur, the disrupter, the obstructionist, the shrinking violet, the efficient worker—an endless list. She suffered from information overload on agents. That whole concept initially paralyzed her with paranoia but Ilse was maturing fast through the hard knocks of politics. Agents were an occupational hazard. But she still couldn't come to grips with poisonous women like Olive. Olive was forever trying to sleep with her. Devious to a fault, the unpleasant creature had devised the perfect method for getting 'nice' women to go to bed with her. She declared all attraction was based on socially conditioned values. Partially true, Ilse conceded, but more so for heterosexuals than lesbians. Olive would either coo or storm depending on the nature of the woman she was about to ensnare. The rap had an ugly familiarity about it. If a woman didn't find Olive sexually attractive, an easy conclusion to arrive at, then Olive declared that the woman was responding out of male values. How could she be a sister? All sisters were to love each other. Therefore, hit the hay. When Olive bore down on Ilse months ago, Ilse cooly avoided her until the rat took up an entire meeting of their political group of twenty women, ranting and raving about how she couldn't work with someone she couldn't trust and how could she work with Ilse because she didn't trust Ilse. And she didn't trust Ilse because she wouldn't sleep with her. Sex predicates trust. Ilse called her a sexual fascist, and the whole room nearly blew up. Back in those days the group divided its loyalties. Half of the women were so gullible or so well trained in niceness they actually sympathized with Olive. As the months wore on even the nicest of women came to understand that Olive was one fucked-up woman. Now all she had left were two devoted followers who were born to be go-fors anyway. People like Olive made Ilse sometimes think in her more bitter moments that the women's movement ought to be called Neurotics Anonymous. But she knew any movement for social change will draw malcontents as well as dedicated women. What puzzled her when she thought about the people she knew in the various feminist groups was that they fell into two camps: the Olives of the world and the women who were gifted, driving, smart. There were no mediocre women. Maybe that was an answer in itself but Ilse, true to her own upper-middle-class Boston background, wanted an analytical jewel. No one she knew listened to you unless you could prove everything you said. Not only did she have an emotional need to explain, she was forced to. Ilse was taught at such an early age to justify she didn't know anything else. She was lively, far more spontaneous than most women her age out of her background, but still she was bound by linear thought. Her message was Dionysian. Her method Apollonian. Curious that she had attracted Carole who seemed on the surface so one-sided, so disciplined, so urbane, all reason. But, Ilse reminded herself, Carole's not repressed or controlled in bed. The older woman fascinated her partly because she was older. Here people vomited forth their entire emotional histories within fifteen minutes of being introduced to you. She'd spent some intense time with Carole and the woman hadn't uttered one word about heavy changes. And all she knew about her past was that she graduated from Vassar in 1951. Curious. Ilse was looking forward to seeing Carole tonight. She wondered what her apartment looked like. Would it be hopelessly bourgeois? Olive Holloway reached over for a finished pamphlet and managed to conveniently linger in Ilse's lap.

"Fuck!" Olive screamed.

Ilse shot her in the breast with the power stapler.

Louisa May Allcat and The Great Pussblossom rushed out to rub against Carole as soon as she opened the door to her apartment. Louisa May thumped down the carpeted stairs of the brownstone to the next floor and then raced back up again. Pussblossom had torn all the toilet paper off the roll and

43

carried half of it onto Carole's prized campaign desk. Carole fed them, picked up the t.p., read her mail, and then opened her folder, eager to pick up her work on "Pagan Images in *Tres Riches Heures du Duc du Berry*." She lost herself in the voluptuous blues, turbulent reds, the purity of color in the Middle Ages. Even the Latin was refreshing after the tough prose of Tacitus or the monotony of Virgil. Some people paid analysts. Carole read Latin and it calmed her. She didn't start out to be a medievalist. Initially, the Renaissance attracted her—once she got into college with the help of a rare scholarship from Vassar plus gifts of money from Richmond's Daughters of the Confederacy, Catholic women, and others she forgot. But she didn't forget the Fan during the Depression and the hot Richmond Septembers when she'd trudge back to school and concentrate on her studies because she knew it was her only hope. Her mother used to tell her she'd be a movie star because she was so beautiful. But even if it weren't the pitiable dream of an impoverished woman saddled with a husband crippled in World War I, even if it could have happened, Carole would have never become an actress. She was going to use her head. She told herself that over and over again, every time she looked at the desolate houses that comprised the poor white district. After that, Vassar and the Renaissance flashed before her like a dream come true. Here intellect was respected. Here women came to learn, to seriously apply their minds, and didn't the Renaissance symbolize that great burst in Western life? So she thought. But as she entered her senior year and began the agonizing process of filling out applications for graduate school, form after form for fellowships, grants, scholarships, any kind of money, a wizened professor, Miss McPherson, told her to forget the Renaissance as a field. Women couldn't advance there, she said. Try antiquity or the Middle Ages. It was a matter-of-fact statement, a weather report with no explanation and Carole, respectful of the old woman, wouldn't have dreamed of asking for one. At first she thought Professor McPherson wanted her to get into the Middle Ages because the old lady spent her career trying to rehabilitate the reputation of a tenth century nun, Hrotsvitha of Gandershiem. And Miss McPherson was a classicist not an art historian. But as fellowships were the heart of the matter the professor who liked her so much was honestly trying to help. Carole changed her field and it paid off. She hated the other medievalists at graduate school. What a dry lot. At least the people laboring under the shadow of Athens or Rome possessed a sense of humor, a glimmer of life. But she stuck it out and gradually another vision of lusty, violent, pious, contradictory people emerged and she found herself entranced by them. Adele had once explained the reason she got into the pre-Columbian period: "I became fascinated with those ancient stone faces peering enigmatically from the past." So it was for her—a vivid, piercing recognition that once, seven hundred years ago, the dead were flesh and her flesh depended on their prior existence. Over the years she shied from departmental politics and withdrew more and more to contemplation of this other time. Her articles were incisive, revealing. She made a name for herself, was recognized as an authority. And she knew, thanks to old Professor McPherson, that one of the reasons was that men didn't invade the field in huge numbers.

If I were Ilse's age, she asked herself, would I make the same choice? The pressures are different now. Those young people I saw at Mother Courage have many more opportunities than we did. But I'd still be drawn to the past, to beauty, to concrete proof that even in our worst times we sought to make at least one thing beautiful, a chapel, a manuscript, a cloak. I'm not sure those women in their workshirts and little enamel stars understand that or even want to understand. Were I twenty-one today I'd make the same choice again. I'd still do it alone I guess, alone but for the help of Miss McPherson. She looked down at the first page of her paper:

The Roman Empire in its decline withdrew from England and Western Europe like a great river receding, leaving small puddles of Latin, of learning, in the rough lands it had formerly conquered.

She knew her work was good and she was glad to be alive.

"Then what happened?" Carole implored, reaching over to grab another pickled egg. "Delicious, Dell, give me this recipe before I go."

"It's Pennsylvania Dutch. Oh, yes, well it seems BonBon and Creampuff pulled every string they had ... "

"Adele, that was a bad one."

Adele threw her head back and howled. "That one was so bad, honey, I didn't even know about it." The plain red turtleneck brought out Adele's best skin tones and she wore a necklace of orange beads interspersed with tigers' teeth. "Well, in fact, it's the truth, they did pull every string they had to get Maryann the runner-up or second lead or whatever you call it in this traveling tent show. God knows where she is now but last night she was in Maryland right outside of Washington, D. C., and whoever was there will never forget it."

"If you don't get to the point I'll open that damn bird cage and tie you under your Montezuma water wall!" Carole raised her voice and Lester thought it was his cue.

"Bwana, White Devil! Bwana, White Devil!" he shrieked at the top of his little lungs.

"Not now, Lester, Mother's talking," Adele called over her shoulder.

He put his crest down and shifted his weight from foot to foot.

"Okay, now in fairness to Maryann we have to admit she can sing a bit."

"Agreed," Carole said.

"She's in 'The Music Man' playing a prim and proper character singing a song or two."

"She is acting."

"According to BonBon, when you're working the tents you wear battery packs taped to some part of your body where it doesn't show. You know, for the mikes. Maryann was wired for sound. She had an ariel running down the small of her back and another wire up to her lavalier."

"Sounds dirty but I thought a lavalier was something dangling from your neck with Kappa Alpha Theta at the end of it."

"Close enough. That's what they call those little

microphones you wear like a necklace. And they have switches so you can turn the sound on or off. If you're going off stage for a costume change or whatever you turn your pack off otherwise everyone will hear what's going on."

"I think I know what's coming. She walked backstage, started with her blue language and then stepped back on stage as River City's bastion of morality."

"Carole, it's worse." Adele's sides were already heaving and she reached over and put her hand on Carole's forearm, paused, then lowered her voice to try and keep from exploding. "Maryann exited all right and forgot to turn off her pack while she walked into the bathroom and let fly. It must have sounded like the '1812 Overture' and she was making it worse by talking to herself about it while she was on the can. Honey, when that child walked back on the stage the entire audience suffered a fit of mass hysteria. And no one in the cast had the heart to tell her what happened for fear she'd be too mortified to continue. For the rest of the evening the audience laughed every time she even so much as breathed. Maryann thought she had comic genius because she received a standing ovation at curtain call. Wasn't until she took her make-up off that the woman playing Marion the librarian, oh what's her name, some Hollywood star exhumed from the fifties? Well, it's not important. But the great lady felt upstaged by a bowel movement so she informed Maryann in no uncertain terms to turn her pack off or she'd shove it up her ass which would certainly put an end to her troubles."

"Adele, stop. You're making my stomach hurt I'm laughing so hard."

48

The two of them made so much noise that Lester started up again.

"Bwana, Bwana. White Devil. Balls, said the queen. If I had two I'd be king. If I had four I'd be a pinball machine. Bwana!"

"Cool it, bird," Adele sputtered trying to catch her breath.

By now the community of birds was in an uproar and Lester sang, "Everybody's doing it, doing it."

"Damn that LaVerne. She's been teaching Lester vulgar rhymes and he loves them."

"I'm going into the bathroom to get a kleenex. After that tale I have to blow my nose and wipe my eyes."

"Carole, be sure your battery pack is turned off."

"I'm coming right back. No show tonight."

"Doing it, doing it, picking their nose and chewing it, chewing it." Lester was wound up.

"Stop it. Do you hear me? Stop it." Adele shook her finger in his face and he shifted from foot to foot again, enjoying the attention.

The mynah attempted a song but Lester out-shouted him, "Doing it, doing it. Bwana. Ack. Bwana."

"Professor Hanratty, do something about this bird you inflicted upon me."

"Maybe if we go back to the coffee table and ignore them all they'll settle down. Right, Lester?"

Lester stopped his rhymes and was now into jungle calls.

"That's an amazing sound. I've never heard him do that before."

"For all I know that could be his natural call but

with Lester nothing is natural. He probably picked it up off a Tarzan movie or LaVerne's been coaching him again behind my back."

"I'm eating another one of these eggs." Carole plucked one out of the white bowl with her left hand, keeping her coke at the ready with her right. "So did Maryann quit in a moment of embarrassment?"

"Maryann? Leave that role as the mayor's wife? She opens the refrigerator door and does twenty minutes."

Lester had calmed down to an occasional screech although he muttered, "Balls, said the queen," a few times in a low voice.

"How's your paper coming?" Adele inquired.

"Sensational, I think. I'm essentially finished with it except for polishing the writing itself."

"Am I going to get to read it?"

"Of course. Would I submit something for publication without the scrutiny of my most esteemed colleague?"

"That's right," Adele answered, her mouth full of egg. "M-m-m." She swallowed. "Today I got a call from that young guy down at University of Pennsylvania and he wants me to go on his dig in the Yucatan next summer, all expenses paid."

"Oh, Dell, that's wonderful." Carole put her coke down, got up, and just missed slamming into the coffee table in her haste to get to Adele sitting in the huge wing chair. She hugged and kissed her. "God, that's exciting. Have you told Verne?"

"No, I thought I'd wait until she gets home and tell her in person. I know she'll be happy for me but she won't want to spend close to three months alone next summer.

"Maybe she can take a few extra weeks off around vacation time and join you."

"That's what I hope she'll do. Since we know this early, she can make arrangements at work. They love her at Bloomies anyway and you know LaVerne, she'll come back with a whole line of something hot from Central America. That girl's a fortune teller. She senses what people will buy. She's usually a year ahead of *Women's Wear Daily*."

"True. While I'm up want anything from the kitchen? I'm getting another coke."

"Yeah, bring me a coke too and potato chips. I feel like shit food."

"Okay."

Carole's activities in the kitchen attracted Lester's attention, particularly when she opened the noisy potato chip bag, and he chattered a whole row of something unintelligible although the last word was distinctly *snot*.

"Here's your drink. What's that on the record player? With all the commotion around this place I didn't hear it."

"LaBelle. Remember when LaVerne and I took you to the Baths? This was the group singing there."

"They were heaven," Carole recalled. "What a wild night."

"How's Ilse?"

"Fine. She's responsible for a big dance at the Firehouse tonight so she's busy with that."

"Been about two months now, hasn't it, that you've been seeing her? You getting serious?" Adele looked directly at Carole.

"She's likeable and you know the attraction between us is incendiary. I'm getting a crash course in women's liberation though. I could do without some of that. Anyway, Adele, if I were serious you'd know about it."

"Sometimes people are in deeper than they realize."

"I don't know. I don't know if that's happening. I'm wary. There are times when it's *deja vu*. Here she is saying something that's absolutely a new thought to her but it's the same thing we said or went through twenty years ago."

"I hate to admit it but there do seem to be phases, stages of life."

"I'm beginning to think we're all conscripts of civilization." A wry smile appeared on Carole's face.

Adele pointed a finger at her, "Conscripts or not, oppressed or free, honey, the conspiracy of the living is to help one another carry on."

"Adele, you're marvelous."

Adele nodded. "Yeah, I even think so myself, sometimes."

"If Ilse were here she'd say you should think that all the time. Women have a low self-image, too little ego. We need to bring that out in each other. I get so bored with the stuff Ilse tells me to read—fallopian tubes, ovaries, uteruses. Jesus christ, I'm not interested in my plumbing."

"I read the 'Woman-Identified Woman' paper you passed on to me. Made a lot of sense but then it was written by lesbians. I can only take the doomed-by-our-ovaries ladies for so long myself and most of the other stuff I've looked at all had that complaint qual-

52

ity about it. And the incredible emphasis on sex, gay or straight. Maybe it's their age or maybe it's that the more repressed you are the more interesting sex is as a topic. All I know is I don't want to hear it."

Carole sighed, "I know. Half of the stuff she gives me to read is so badly written or run off so fuzzy I can't make it out. Doesn't apply to me or to you. I don't feel inferior to men. I can't remember ever feeling inferior. I knew as a kid that boys got all the breaks but it made me mad—just made me fight that much harder. I'm not sitting home with three bawling kids and I have other things to do besides complain about how awful men are. Bores the hell out of me."

"Surely since Ilse's a lesbian herself she understands we're different from housewives. I don't know though—maybe there are housewives who are lesbians. Let's face it, we pushed for careers. I suspect a straight woman our age with a good career feels a lot like we do." Adele furrowed her eyebrows.

Carole stalled a moment. "She thinks lesbians are the vanguard of the women's movement but I think she sees all women as victims. She happens to see us as the strongest women. But she has an excuse to cover everybody's failure or special bitch. It's male supremacy or capitalism or racism. I get them mixed up."

"They are mixed up."

"Dell, I never was interested in politics and a women's movement doesn't make me any more interested in politics than before. I think politics is the framework of a nation, fundamental, but I'm interested in interior decorating not carpentry, know what I mean?"

"We'd better look out or the house will fall down."

"Ha. You're right but I still can't work up enthusiasm for the subject. You know, I would have been head of the department if I weren't a woman; hell, I'm still not a full professor. I hate all that. But what's most important to me is to do my work and I happen to think that work is important. How can I do my work if I'm on some picket line or down at the women's center answering telephones? You tell me?"

"Obviously, you can't. But I can tell you this," Adele stated.

"What?"

"The ideas of the movement are getting to you. You wouldn't be questioning yourself, your work, if you didn't feel some pull."

"That's ridiculous." Carole waved her hand.

"Uh huh."

"Adele, stop sitting there like a Cheshire cat."

"You don't have to defend yourself to me but you ought to take a step back and see that Ilse is more important to you than you're admitting and what she stands for is having its effect. To even consider the ideas is some fragile kind of involvement."

"Sometimes I think you know me better than I know myself."

"What are you doing on September twenty-ninth?" Adele shifted gears.

"Nothing, why?"

"How would you like a date with destiny?"

"Sounds mysterious."

Try as she would Carole couldn't ferret out of Adele what was going to happen on September twenty-ninth. All Adele would tell her was to get gussied up and be ready by seven in the evening.

Carole stayed on an hour after that. She and Adele never ran out of things to talk about. Then she walked home, sorting her clothes out in her head. She promised Ilse she'd come to the dance tonight and she had no idea what to wear. But then she remembered it really wasn't that important. Ilse didn't pay much attention to her clothes. She was in too big a hurry to get them off.

Wooster Street lies in the heart of Soho where the narrow streets prevent the ugly, light-manufacturing buildings from running into each other. Many of the buildings were reclaimed in the late sixties, early seventies, by artists searching for cheap space, a commodity in ever-diminishing supply in the bursting city. The idea quickly caught on and inside those grimy exteriors flourished magnificent lofts enriched by the particular talent of their owners. The Firehouse sitting in the middle of the block had been converted for use by gay political groups.

Carole sprung out of the fat Checker cab and thought she'd be run over by a fire truck—the place hadn't been touched on the outside. The door hung open to let a little air in the three-story building. Music blared into the deserted street and bounced off the buildings in a muffled echo. The smoke inside was so thick Carole couldn't see much except the two women behind a table at the door. She paid her two-dollar donation, ventured in, and gave up on ever locating Ilse. A winding, metal staircase was to her right, a literature table took up space underneath it and, behind the table, basement steps were jammed with people running up and down getting drinks. Beyond that was a long space mobbed with women. There were women in workshirts, women in sequined halters; there were women in old band uniforms and women in no shirts at all. The place was such a racial mix that Carole might have thought she was at a gathering of the United Nations' employees except for the fact that they were all dancing with each other. That and how would the United Nations react to bare breasts?

She'd never find Ilse but she might as well try. As she plunged through the gyrating hundreds she became acutely conscious of the fact that she was a good fifteen years older than the oldest of them.

God, I'm glad I wore my jeans, she thought. She also wore one of LaVerne's Nik-Nik blouses but considering the heat of all these pressed bodies and the new dress code, it didn't matter. Her height and firm body turned many a head as she wandered through. The dim light softened her deep laugh lines and she could have passed for thirty-four, if she cared about looking young which she didn't. Her first gray hair appearing at age twenty-three didn't reconcile her to the inevitability of age. She remembered her mother joking that no one minded getting older, they minded looking older. But she didn't understand that she was going to age like her mother did in Richmond, like Grams did up in the foothills before Winchester; not until Margaret's death did she understand that simple fact.

Bumping into the young bodies touching each other in celebration of the night, each other their youth, Carole slid back into time, toward a turning point in her own youth. Surrounded by strangers she was pulled back by a slumbrous undertow, back into a time when she knew no other world but the world of the young, innocence laced with ignorance. She returned to the moment when she learned what we each must learn. She was twenty-five years old, soon to be twenty-six.

"Adele, this paper is going to do it for you. I just know it."

"You mean get me up and over?"

"I just know it will. I don't know much about your field but this paper on Olmec vestiges in Mayan art reads like a Dorothy Sayers mystery. It's exciting. What have you read in art history lately that's exciting?"

"Yeah, well, that's it. They're such damned stuffed shirts. I'm hesitant to turn this in."

"Oh, come on, take the chance. What the hell. If they don't like it we'll start searching out hospitable universities that will appreciate you. Any school that's too dumb to see the value of this paper, both content and style, doesn't deserve to have you."

"Are you for hire?" Adele poked her ribs. "Speaking of hire, we'd better get our asses out on the street and find a cab or we'll never make it to Lynn Feingarten's party and you know she's got this thing for you."

"She can keep her thing to herself."

"What? I thought you fancied her ever so slightly."

"Oh, we had dinner a few times but honest to god, Dell, if Lynn were a man she'd be a regimental-tie queen, you know what I mean?"

"Yes, I know what you mean. But darlin', half of

57

New York City is busy being oh-so-refined."

"I can't bear it. Remember what Chanel said, 'Luxury is not the absence of poverty but the absence of vulgarity.' "

"Ha, Feingarten does glitter with all that jewelry. You ought to tell her."

"Tell her nothing. I say let's throw her in the Hudson. Every fish within five miles will come after all that shiny stuff."

"Honey, you are getting downright venomous. What'd she do to you?"

"Two things. First she made a pass that was so crude it defies description. I can't stand that lady-butch crap. Second, and worse, far the worse, she said I had a Southern accent and I'd be far more attractive if I lost it. The nerve of that overdressed tart."

"There is a delicate bouquet of magnolia in your speech."

"Adele, I slaved like a cotton-picker to get rid of that when I was at school."

"Yes, well, it's coming out now. Besides, Scarlett, my folks were the cotton pickers, remember?"

"Like hell they were. Your grandfather probably sold them all snake-oil to get rid of the aches and pains. That's how your family got so disgustingly rich." Carole howled.

Adele giggled. "Now don't you be telling anyone such horrible lies about me. My Granddaddy made a fortune selling Black folks creme to lighten their skin."

At this outrageousness Carole screamed, "Adele, ninety per cent of the terrible things they say about you are untrue but ten per cent is worse than anyone can imagine!"

"That's right. Don't you forget it."

"Your grandfather didn't do that, really, did he?"

"Of course not but it's such a good lie. You want to know how we got the money, cross my heart?"

"Seeing as we've known each other for around six years now, I'd love to know."

"Didn't your mother tell you talking about money is trash?"

"Yeah but that's because we didn't have any to talk about and neither did anyone else so why embarrass all your friends."

Adele relished this. "Now see, I was told the exact same thing for opposite reasons. Anyway, Grandfather did start the business rolling and it's stayed in the family ever since. As a chemist at the turn of the century he developed a line of beauty aides for colored people as he still calls us and it's boomed ever since. Dad went into law, has Grandfather's account and a lot of other fat accounts as well as real estate. My father is a shrewd man. He can smell money in a clover blossom."

"God knows there are many ways to make a buck and I haven't discovered one. Must be what I inherited from all those generations of poverty." Carole laughed.

"Oh, you're doing pretty good for a single woman."

"I know but academic types rarely get rich."

"But we have time—time to think, travel, read, write. That's a greater luxury to me than money which incidentally I could have had. I know Granddad would give me that business. Of all the grandchildren he loves me the best because he says I'm the smartest. Shows you what he knows," she grinned.

"I don't know, Dell. It would be a challenge, don't you think?"

"Sure it would but not for me. Anyway, when everyone dies at age a hundred and ten I'll get my share then I'll fund a dig, so help me, I will. Think of that, my own Mayan city!"

"Hope you're not too old to enjoy it by the time you get the loot."

"Listen, Hanratty, I intend to be a mean old woman and live forever."

The phone rang and Carole slowly got to her feet. "I'll bet it's Lynn F. insisting in her best Tallulah voice that we get over there. Think of some little white lie."

"I will not. You make up your own lies. Oh let's go. I'm in the mood for a party."

Carole picked up the phone. "Carole, Carole this is Mother."

"Mother?"

"Honey, I have bad news." Her voice was quite deliberate; she pronounced each word evenly as if it were a keystone, as if any word that got lost in emotion would make the whole weight of the sentence fall apart and crush her. "Can you hear me?"

"Yes, yes, I can hear you. The connection is clear. Mother, what's wrong?"

"Margaret was in a three-way accident down by the Capitol."

Carole began to shake. Adele came over to her and stood helplessly not knowing what to do. Carole looked up at her.

"Mother, where is she? How is she?"

"Honey, she's gone. Burned. She was hit from behind and the gas tank blew. There's nothing left." Still the voice stayed firm if weak.

"Mom, I'll catch the next train out. I'll get there as fast as I can."

"Yes, come home, honey. You come on home." On the word *home* she cried, quietly. "Now I have to hang up. Do you have anyone with you? I don't want you alone until you leave."

"I have a friend here, Adele."

"That's a nice name. I don't believe I ever met her." Anything attached to ordinary exchange seemed to comfort the older woman.

"No, Mother, you haven't met her. Now you hang up. Is Luke there to take care of you?"

"Luke's right here next to me, honey. You come home."

"I'll see you tomorrow, Mom. Goodbye."

"I can't say that." She cried harder now and hung up the phone.

"Carole, what in the world is wrong?"

"My sister, Margaret, was killed in a car accident." Carole's lip trembled. When Adele put her arms around her she couldn't see for crying. Adele guided her over to the sofa. She didn't try to say anything. Words were useless. Carole cried for three-quarters of an hour. She couldn't stop herself. It got so bad she got the dry heaves and a splitting headache. Slowly she stopped crying. Finally she spoke, "We were more like twins than sisters."

"You told me about her many times . . . I am so sorry, baby, I'm just so sorry."

"Adele, you're awful good." Carole hugged her again and cried some more. They rocked back and forth until she quieted herself. "I've got to go pack."

"You tell me what you want and I'll pack."

"No, I have to do something, anything."

"I'll call the train station then."

A train left late that night for Washington, D. C., where Carole would have to lay over for hours before catching another train to Richmond. Adele, ignoring Carole's protests, rode with her to D. C. and waited through the night to put her on her connection to Richmond. They nibbled donuts and talked of life and death and how they never believed it could happen to them. Carole couldn't sleep and Adele wouldn't, so the hours, like a magic circle, closed around them and strengthened the bond of friendship already between them. As Carole boarded the train, finally, she turned to Adele and said, "You're my sister now," and before Adele could answer she ran up the steps and into the train.

Richmond, like an ageing empress, surviving her emperor, glowed on the Virginia landscape. Other Southern cities surpassed her. They were bigger, livelier, lovelier, but children of the South still paid homage to the Capital of the Confederacy. A grandmother who had seen siege, death, and defeat, she dispensed her wisdom to anyone with eyes. Generations later the scars intertwined with new roads, new buildings, but Richmond's wounds were never completely healed. The South was and remains a battered nation. Richmond will always rest next to the deepest of those wounds. As Carole walked the platform toward her waiting brother, Luke, Richmond filled her, opened her own very personal wound. It was as though she had never left this place and yet it was different. Luke walked down to her, kissed her, picked up her bags, and drove her home in his pride and joy, a 1955 Chevy, only three years old.

The usual funeral extravaganza made Carole all the more determined to die on a remote island where no human could embarrass her into the afterlife. Smothered as the casket was with gladiolas, Carole swore she could smell burned flesh. Such nearness to death in its tactile form terrified her. Margaret, sparkling, so pretty, so full of the devil, reduced to unrecognizable, stinking meat.

Mother bore the whole social consequences of death with dignity. Carole stood by her, wondering at the woman's patience. You can only hear tidings of consolation repeated so many times before you're ready to snatch the damned black veils off their shining hats and stuff them in their mouths. Luke stayed mute for the proceedings. Overwhelmed by emotion he took a typical male retreat and drank alarming quantities of whiskey. He was of no use whatsoever to Mother. She bore him as well as her sadness. Carole stayed on a week, looking after her mother and finally smashing all of Luke's damned bottles of booze on the side of his 1955 Chevy. Half in the bag Luke heard the tinkling of glass and roared out of the house.

"What in the goddamned hell do you think you're doing, Carole Lee?"

"Are you so snookered you can't see?"

"I'll go buy more," her older brother flared.

"And I'll smash every damn one I find."

"I ought to wipe that smile off your face."

"Go ahead, asswipe. You can beat me up but brother I am going to hurt you bad while you do it."

Luke shifted, his arms dropped to his sides. He was eight years older than his sister. Margaret had been three years older than Carole. A World War II veteran, Luke was an American contradiction: he worshipped violence but he feared death. Margaret's death upset him more than the organized brutality of his infantry days in the European theater. That was war and bad as it was Luke had a place for it. But Margaret, a sister he loved, a sister he helped raise—the death of that adored person was beyond him. He had no place for such pain and no one warned him such a pain existed.

"Did you scratch my car, you little shit?"

"Come and see for yourself, turd."

At the sound of the word *turd* Luke had to laugh. Both his sisters stood up to him but Carole dipped more frequently into the English language for insults. At least this feigned hostility was better than the pain—for a while, anyway.

"You watch your mouth, Dr. Smartass. Women aren't supposed to talk like that. Shows what comes of going up there with those damn Yankees."

"I swore long before I became an immigrant."

"H-m-m, you're lucky this car ain't scratched."

"How about letting me drive it? I'll take you for a little ride, hero."

With a shift of the gears they rambled down the streets and Carole turned toward the rich side of town where she loved to ride along and look at how the other half lived.

"Luke, you must stop drinking. I've got to go back tomorrow and return to work. Mother needs you sober. You hear me?"

Luke grunted.

"You got a mouth, use it."

"I hear you for christ's sake. I hear you. I don't need you telling me I'm an asswipe. I already know it."

"Lukie, look at that house. My gawd, a small battalion could live in there. Can you imagine living like that?"

"Ah, shit, Carole, that ain't nothing. You should see them castles in Europe. Now that's the way to live."

"While you were knocking the Nazis to hell maybe you should have liberated one little castle for yourself and the family."

"Yeah."

"Hey, what's this little microphone here by the steering wheel."

"Pick it up and say something evil in it and find out."

"You're nuts. Is this another one of your jokes?"

"No, now come on. Say something—wait until we pass this old toad on the corner up there."

As they approached the white-haired gentleman, Carole, at her brother's urging, spoke one of their favorite childhood insults: "Fartblossom."

To her amazement and acute discomfort the offending word blared for all the world to hear and heaven, too. The old man's jaw fell like the gangplank of an amphibious landing craft.

"Luke!" Carole hit the gas and sped from the

scene of her crime.

"Here give it to me."

"Oh, no, you don't. I know what you'll do. Luke, gimme that back. Gimme that."

"Giving you nothing."

Always clever with tools, Luke had engineered loudspeakers next to his horns. To his eternal delight he could wreck anyone's composure.

"Watch me buzz this fucking Cadillac up here. Hey, you. Hey, you in that piece of expensive shit. Move over. Yes, you in the blue Cadillac, this is Richmond's new police aerial control unit talking to you. You're violating code number 84A. Pull over, an officer is on his way to greet you. Don't try to run away. We have your license plate number."

The driver of the automobile pulled over and stuck his head out the window looking for this new, low flying craft. As the little Chevy rolled down the road he still sat there waiting for the police. Luke bellowed, slapping his muscular thigh. "Dumb, dumb. God, people are so dumb if you wrapped up shit in red cellophane they'd buy it. Lookit that rich bastard he's still sitting there." His face shone red with victory and laughter.

"Luke, you beat all. Now gimme that back."

"I'm not giving it to you. I'm gonna have me some fun."

"Give it to me. I promise to play."

"You expect me to believe that?"

"Honest, Luke. See that middle-aged lady walking up there in the feathered hat?"

"Yes, I see her. I ain't blind."

"You say you're the voice of God and talk low

like the preacher. I'll go slow. Then when you're done sanctifying her, give me the microphone."

Luke got so excited as they approached their target, his voice hit his shoes. "Sister. Sister, this is the voice of the Lord calling to thee. Do thee read me, sister?"

Carole winced on the word *read*. "This isn't a bombing mission."

Luke took the hint. "Sister, do thee hear the voice of the Lord, thy God, the Lord of Hosts, the Father of the Lamb?"

The woman's pink hat bobbed up and down with recognition. As they still had not drawn even with her they couldn't observe the look of wonder on her round face.

"Sister of the pink hat I have shown myself to thee to tell thee, thee—yes, thee, thee—good woman, must save this godless country. Turn thy brethren from the worship of Mammon, turn thy brethren towards the path of righteousness. Consider thy past life as blackness, as Jonah swallowed by the whale of greed, selfishness, and spitefulness. Now come forth, good woman, come forth and spread my message to all America."

Coasting past the struck woman they noticed a look of utter shock. Luke started to giggle but he had the good sense to put his hand over the microphone.

"Sister, if thee will do my will fall on thy knees and praise my glory."

She sank down like a shot doe, threw her hands over her head and ripped off a quavering, "Praise be the Lord."

Carole snatched the microphone from Luke's paw

and put the frosting on the cake. "Sister, this is the angel Carole speaking to thee now. Obey the message of the Lord, thy God. Save this nation from sin and destruction. I am leaving thee now, sister, to struggle with the Prince of Darkness and his servants. Sing along with me as my voice fades. No, no, down on thy knees, sister, don't get up yet. As my voice fades, remember thou hast been touched by the Lord." Carole, in a surprisingly spiritual voice, sang "Nearer My God to Thee" and as they turned the corner, there she was down on her knees, hands clasped to her ample bosom, singing the hymn, sweat running over her forehead.

Hysterical with glee, sister and brother drove back home barely in control of the car or themselves. As they pulled in front of the run-down but clean house, Carole punched her brother in the arm, "Jesus, that was fun!"

"I bet that woman starts a tent show right on that very spot." Luke doubled over and said before he realized it, "Shit, I wish Margie could have seen that."

"Oh, hell, she'd of passed herself off as Virgin Mary."

"Yeah, I know." Luke turned to Carole with tears in his eyes. She put her arms around him and kissed him gently on the cheek.

The next day as Luke saw her off he vowed, "No more boozing, Sis. I'll take care of the old girl. You come on home more often. I mean it." He was as good as his word.

On the long ride back to New York she thought of her brother and the price men paid for being men. She thought of Luke's gentleness and sense of humor.

He looked like a grizzly bear and used his fearsome image to ward off others from seeing what rested within him, an incredible sweetness. Of all three of us, Luke is most like Mom, she thought. Margaret tiptoed into her thoughts. Margaret, the dark-eyed, the imaginative, the shining imp as bright as a dragonfly— we Americans want happy endings and death denies us a happy ending. I've rejected death all my life but you, Margaret, true to yourself as in life, made me see how silly I am. It will come to me too just as it came to you, my adorable, big sister. Carole leaned against the window and saw the reds and yellows of the fall. The East Coast bedecked itself before wearing the subtle clothing of wintertime. Reeling from the impact of the color, Carole thought against her will for she no longer wanted to think, "She'll never see this. Why? Why? I don't understand it. I can't understand it. Why should Margaret die? Why should any of us die? What a cruel joke. Well, I'll live double. I'll live for Margaret and me. I'll live for every young and bright and laughing person cut down before her time. If there's a secret of the dead come back to me and tell me, Margaret. If there's a secret of life, oh tell me. Knowing or not knowing, I shall live, I will live, I must live. Life is the principle of the universe. Life!"

Exhausted by this undisplayed emotion she fell asleep and did not awake until the conductor nudged her. "New York City, Miss."

When Carole drowsily collected her luggage and trudged out of the hissing train she saw, to her surprise, a waiting Adele, arms full of flowers, books and records. That was one of the happiest moments of her entire life.

Bumped by a woman with frizzy hair and silver stars painted all over her face, Carole crashed back into the present, astonished at her journey. She put her arms around her body more to convince herself she really was here in 1976 in this scene of colliding costumes, than to keep them out of the way. Yes it was the present, vividly so. No time in the past could have ever looked like this. As her fingers grazed her rib cage she realized how finely made she was. For one second she could trade places with Ilse, sensing what it must be to touch these ribs, the muscled abdomen, the miracle of the flesh.

"We've got to stop meeting this way." Ilse kissed her.

"You've been watching too many old movies," Carole said, glad to see her.

"No, I'm imitating you."

"Your dance is a huge success."

"It always is. We do it every other week. This was my turn to take it on; you know, rotation."

"Do you have to stay through the whole thing?"

"No, I made all the preparations and womaned the door for a couple hours. Jean O'Leary will take care of the tail end."

"Will she be able to shoo them out?"

"So many of these women have a crush on her they'll hang around. Maybe I should go home and bring back my recorder so I can pipe them out. Do you want to go right away or can we dance a bit?"

"Let's go."

"Okay. I've spent too much time here the last few weeks as it is."

Louisa May Allcat zoomed down the stairs and leisurely trotted back up again, satisfied with her routine of escape.

"Louisa, don't be slow about it. In the house."

Naturally, Carole's urging produced the opposite effect and the animal sat down on the third step from the top, content in her ability to irritate.

"Ilse, hold the door a second. Louisa May's getting grand again. The later I come home the longer she sits out there."

Carole scooped up the rotund beast and put her down by her dish. Louisa May revelled in the attention and at the sound of a food dish rattling, a sleepy Pussblossom emerged from under the sofa. Ilse patted her vertical tail and looked around the apartment. As many times as she'd come here, Ilse couldn't get used to it. The place was too thought out, too lush. Although far more imaginative than her parents' home in Brookline, Massachusetts, there was something in the completeness of the apartment that bothered her. The front room looked out on 73rd Street, the windows had shutters on them from the original time of the building's construction, which must have been around 1890. An oriental rug warmed the floor. A beige nineteen-thirties sofa with huge curling arms was flanked on either side by two beige Barcelona chairs. A glass and chrome coffee table positioned between the sofa and chairs had on it one pink chambered nautilis cut in half to reveal the flawless, pearly chambers. An upturned, polished tortoise shell served as an ashtray. The subtle color scheme drew her eyes to the wall, where color blazed. A magnificent feathered flag from Peru hung on one wall, the deep green and teal blue throbbing. Adele, who had one herself, had given it to Carole to remind her that the Incas were more civilized in the Middle Ages than the barbarous Westerners. Carole pointed out to Ilse the first time she visited the apartment that, of course, it was not an original. If it were its price would be a handful of rubies, she laughed. This breathtaking work rested between two medieval manuscript pages, the gold glittering and the Latin crisp even now after all these centuries. On the opposite wall hung three paintings by new artists Carole had discovered this year: Betsy Damon, Judy Chicago, and Byrd Swift. The works, startling in conception and execution, harmonized with her flag and manuscript pages.

Ilse couldn't figure how Carole put things together but clearly the older woman possessed an unusual visual imagination. Perhaps it was the naked sensuousness of the room that jarred Ilse.

The apartment had a strange layout. You walked into a tiny hallway and faced an equally tiny kitchen. The front room was to the right and to the left was a wide workroom with a marble fireplace and off that was a small bedroom that also shared space with the bathroom. Ilse loved Carole's workroom. Whenever she came into it she thought she could sit down and write shatterproof position papers for the movement. The fireplace was in the middle of the room and over it hung a huge carnival wheel of chance. The cats loved sitting on top of the fireplace spinning the wheel and listening to the little metal pins tick against the rubber stopper. All the walls, even the walls up to the fireplace, were floor to ceiling bookshelves crammed with books. A polished, simple campaign desk commanded the middle of the room opposite the fireplace. The brass handles shone and the wood seemed deep and rich with the years. Carole used to wonder who had it, Napoleon or Wellington? She wanted to know which side to be on. An impressive unabridged dictionary was left of the desk, on a small podium and within reach. A Smith Corona electric typewriter occupied the right side of the desk and the middle of the smooth surface held two neat piles of papers. A brass inkwell with two Montblanc pens glittered. Even with all the bookshelves, huge stacks of books silently waited on the floor for Carole to build bookshelves all over her bedroom. A big window behind the dictionary looked out into the garden of the apartment below.

Despite her passion for Carole, Ilse always lingered in the workroom before plunging into the small bedroom. Somehow Carole put lights behind a narrow floorboard so light swept across your feet and you felt as though you were floating or walking in mist. A simple double bed was in the center with a deep maroon, crushed-velvet bedspread. Two campaign chests on either side held some clothes and the rest hung in the small closet. Although the walls were bare the floor wasn't. A few curvaceous pieces of sculpture loomed up out of the clouds.

Although exhausted, the responsibility and frenzy of the dance had Ilse speeding. Carole brought her a sandwich and a cold beer. They sat in the living room.

"Everytime I come here this place blows my mind."

"Coming from you I don't know whether that's a

compliment or an insult."

"Well, it's beyond bourgeois. I mean there's so much easiness and class here."

Carole sighed. Ilse was terrified of being comfortable.

"What's wrong with that? I thought that's what people fought revolutions for, to gain some comfort and advantage."

Ilse wiggled out to the edge of her chair. "Not exactly. Freedom is as important, maybe more important."

"That's an elusive concept. Are the Russians free?"

"You can't compare what we want to do with other revolutions. They were male supremacists, remember? We'll go beyond that."

"I remember, but I still don't know what freedom means when anyone says it. In the Middle Ages it meant irresponsibility. Society was a chain of limited privilege that worked to the disadvantage of all but a few. Political freedom meant exemption from the law. In Russia in 1917 it meant the dictatorship of the proletariat and today in America freedom is debased to mean consumer choice. So you tell me what you mean."

Ilse swallowed some beer, cocked her head, and stared at Carole. Did she want to fight or did she want to talk?

"Freedom means the right to choose how you want to live and it means the right to participate in governmental and economic decisions. You're right, there is a confusion between political freedom and material benefits. But, to me, freedom means being able to shape your environment, working with others.

We're all responsible to each other in my concept of freedom."

"That's close enough to my view. I don't know how we go about it but if that's what the movement stands for, how could anyone be against it?"

"The pigs on top are against it. They smear the women's movement as being anti-male so people will be afraid of us, so they won't listen to what we have to say. I'm not letting men off the hook. But holding a man responsible for his part in woman oppression and being anti-male are two different things."

Carole moved forward. "It seems to me you all are strong on analysis of what's wrong and weak on program."

Ilse twitched and put her sandwich on the plate; her voice shot up a bit. "Carole, we're new. I mean we've only existed as a political idea since about 1968. Give us time."

"What do you mean? What do you think the suffragists were doing back at the turn of the century? Even I know that much."

"It's not the same. They wanted to participate in the government. They got screwed up on the vote, you know. I mean they thought the vote was really doing something. They finally got it in 1920 and then the party split. Most of the women said, we have what we want; the smarter ones said, no we don't, we need equal rights. Shit, the damn Equal Rights Amendment still isn't on the Constitution." Ilse was getting impassioned. She couldn't think about the past, even though she wasn't part of it, without seething. "Anyway, that's old stuff. I don't want to participate in this rotten government. I don't want stock in

General Motors. I don't want to get rich off the suffering in Viet Nam. The war's over. What a crummy joke. I want a new government, a democracy, a real government of the people."

Carole touched Ilse on the shoulder to try and soothe her. "Honey, I believe you. I just don't know how it's done."

"Well, it's not done by shutting ourselves off from one another, that old American individualism crap. Maybe that's why this place blows my mind. I mean it's so individual. And why should you pay this much rent? I bet you pay four hundred dollars or more for this place." Frustration at not having an instant plan flushed Ilse's face and she turned on Carole. "And what good does an art historian do anybody, really?"

Stunned by the vehemence of the outburst, Carole dropped her hand. Her impulse was to lash right back but she tried to keep in mind that Ilse was overwrought by a week of strain, that she was twenty years younger, and that she respected the younger woman's commitment even if she didn't always agree with her. Besides, maybe this had been coming on for sometime now.

"Ilse, what good am I to anyone if I go back to the slums? Be reasonable."

"What do you mean go back to the slums?" Ilse doubted her.

"I worked for everything I have. I didn't come from money. Honey, I grew up in the Depression in Richmond, Virginia—one of three kids. We lived in the Fan. It was a slum pretty much, although we didn't call it that ourselves. In the last ten years, since I was thirty-four, I've been able to get things for myself. Up to that time I was paying off loans and helping with my parents' hospital bills until they died. You walk into someone's life and assume their life is static. I worked for this. I've hurt no one in the process and I've helped those closest to me. Why should I be made to feel guilty?"

"You're too sophisticated to come from the slums. Adele maybe but not you," Ilse said in a somewhat softer voice.

"Keep it up and you're going to be a radical celibate."

"Come on, Carole, poor people don't act the way you do."

The fury of being, in essence, called a liar propelled Carole. "Who the hell are you to doubt my word? Who the hell are you to set up standards of behavior for people you don't even know about? How dare you assume poor people are stupid, insensitive, inarticulate!"

"I didn't say that."

"You didn't have to. That's what you implied. Talk about stereotypes. That's as bad as what men do to women. Just because we didn't have anything doesn't mean we spoke fractured English, lived in filth, and fought with regularity every Saturday night. And even if I had lived that way give me, give all people a little credit—we can change, you know. You've complained to me a hundred times how white and middle-class your movement is. Well, no wonder. You've insulted other women. Don't you ever tell me how to act, my dear. Don't you ever revise my past. Leave the revisionists to Russia. There are more differences between poor people than between middle-class people. Don't you know that? I'm different from a poor white woman raised in the fields of South Carolina. You've got one stereotype to fit all of us and when you meet someone who grew up in poverty you can't even recognize her. When you start asking people to justify their past to you, you set it up so they hate you."

"I, uh, didn't know you knew much about Russia."

"For christ's sake, Ilse, I was in my twenties at the height of the Red scare. I made it my business to try and learn a little something. Your generation isn't the only one who's read Marx."

"Oh."

The room vibrated like a lightening rod after it's been struck. Slowly the tension was grounding.

"During the fifties I read stuff about Russian history. To tell you the truth I didn't read Marx until four years ago. The story's actually funny. It was my fortieth birthday, a big day. Adele threw a party for me and afterwards we sat and wound down in her living room. LaVerne started the whole thing. She'd bought some damn stock—software which looked good because of the computer boom. It skyrocketed up and just as quickly fell back to earth with a fat splat. LaVerne nearly died and she was bitching about the economy. I voiced my ignorance about economic matters and Adele said she didn't really know what goes on either. LaVerne is the sharpest of us all and she briefly explained the stock market so it made some sense to me but she said she didn't know how goods go from country to country or what gold had to do with all of it. We sat there and looked at each other, three adult women sitting in the economic dark. So LaVerne suggested we each read a book and tell the others what was in it, like high school book reports. She grabbed Keynes, Adele took Galbraith, and I took Marx. Whizzed through the *Communist Manifesto* and got overconfident. That's when I had a head-on collision with *Das Capital*. Have you ever read it?"

"No, but I've read interpretations and stuff."

"You mean I've read *Capital* and you haven't?" Carole brushed Ilse's cheek.

"Don't tease me." She kissed Carole's hand. "Did you three come to any conclusions?"

"Yes. The rich get richer and the poor get poorer and my mother told me that." Carole laughed.

"You can't resist a good line."

"Ilse, don't be so serious. I absorbed a little about labor, value, utility, accumulation, but economics isn't my field. We read our books. We informed ourselves and each other. I watch what goes on but as I said it's not my field. I'm an alert amateur."

"Are you a Marxist?"

"Who knows. I think Marxists need their own ecumenical council to realign the faithful."

"You're not answering my question."

"The shades of Marxism confuse me. I certainly don't swallow it all. I forget what you call the old line Marxists. I like to think of them as secular Jesuits. Marx did give us a new way to look at the world and I've certainly been taught by him. But he wrote that stuff over a hundred years ago, some of it. We have to take what's useful for us today. You should know me well enough by now, Ilse, to know I don't uncritically accept anything. And as I told you, I'm not an economist. All I know is that when Marx exhorted the workers of the world to lose their chains, I thought, right, so the United States can sell them for junk."

In spite of herself, Ilse laughed. The fight took out her last ounce of energy and she was ebbing just as Carole was picking up.

"Another thing that strikes me when I read is that all political organization seems based on the notion of an outside enemy," Carole bubbled.

"Yeah . . . "

"Not that the Czar wasn't the enemy or even that Dupont isn't now an enemy, I guess, but there's something about that conception that bothers me. It's naive. There's something worse than an outside enemy: an inside enemy."

"Carole, I'm not sure I follow. I'm getting fuzzy."

"Let's go to bed then. Come on." She put her arm around Ilse's waist as they walked into the bedroom. "While I'm thinking about it, let me run this out quickly. We think in these set ways. A Brazilian has a Brazilian way of doing something and a French person has something peculiarly Gallic about him."

"Her," Ilse corrected.

"Her. We operate on ideas that are unquestioned, you see. That's why revolutions fail. Russia still has a czar, of sorts. It might even be possible, and here's where most of your friends will disagree with me, but it might even be possible that some of the unquestioned woman ways aren't good ways. While we're women we're also Americans, aren't we? I'll bet you dollars to donuts your ideas of feminism and how to achieve democracy are very different from your Japanese counterpart."

80

"It's not all that clear to me but what I'm getting sounds right. I don't know how we find out what's unquestioned."

"Travel." Carole slipped into bed and Ilse, her eyes half closed, put her head on the tall woman's shoulder.

"One more thing," Carole continued.

"Huh?"

"Adele comes from one of St. Louis's best families. Her father's a lawyer and the last thing they were was poor."

"Oh," Ilse murmured. "Did you and Adele ever go to bed?"

"No."


Fred Fowler relished the first departmental meeting of the fall semester. Fall was the big semester for him and he thought of each fall as turning over a new leaf. He wasn't a particularly efficient administrator nor did he have direction but when there was no avenue of escape he was capable of tremendous bursts of energy. Since the department ran on a crisis basis, Fred worked hard. The meeting was at three. Fred fussed at his secretary to make certain the ashtrays were on the table and did she have the ice bucket ready? Fred thought liquor brought the group together, oiled the machinery of the department.

Carole breezed out of the elevator door and nearly crashed into him running up and down the hall like an absent-minded track star, first this way then back again.

"Whoops, Professor Hanratty, you leave a dangerous wake."

"Excuse me, Chief, that's the second time today I narrowly averted a crash."

"Goodness, I hope it wasn't serious." He was eager to console her should there be a horror story. Fred was terribly good at playing oh-ain't-it-awful.

"No, nothing like that. As I hurried out of my apartment building I flattened Mr. Dutton who was hurrying in."

Dutton was a snide, fifty-year-old bachelor. Carole was sure he was a gigolo in his younger days, because he had a snotty charm that probably appealed to older, lonesome females. Dutton inhabited the garden apartment. He also minced up and down the East Seventies with his balding pekinese. Smothered in Gucci, the man couldn't abide Carole because she didn't pay attention to him. Worse, one day when he'd let his dog off its leash, it bounded up to the third floor just as Carole opened her apartment door. Louisa May, ready for her great escape, roared out and put on the brakes when she saw the little creature. Once Louisa May figured out it was, in fact, a dog, she huffed up twice her size and pounded the shit out of it. Dutton flew up the stairs, witnessed his dog's bloody nose, and shrilly christened Louisa May a "ferocious predator." If there were any doctor bills to be paid she'd hear about them. Carole figured Dutton would get money out of a woman one way or the other. Today as she smacked into him, his automatic umbrella opened up on him and he stuck in the doorway.

All eight professors in the room, Fred began his fall speech: "Welcome back. I hope each of you had a pleasant and stimulating summer. After we attend to business perhaps Bob Kenin will tell us informally

82

how restoration progresses in Florence." Bob nodded. "As it's our first meeting we have a clean slate except for the controversy within the department over grading. The issue is resolved for undergraduate courses but, as you may recall, our last meeting before the summer semester involved a great deal of concern over this system being employed for our graduate students, our cream of the crop, aha." Nervous smile until ancient Professor Stowa smiled back. "I suggest we read the two papers written by our exponents of the different viewpoints and we can debate the matter two weeks from today. Of course, I don't mean to imply that a debate will settle the matter. Grading is a complex moral issue as well as a matter of protecting the standards of our department, so I feel we're dealing with the tip of the iceberg. Blah, blah, blah."

Tuning out on iceberg, Carole stared at Fred gloating over his self-importance, taking liberal sips of his drink. People reveal how ordinary their minds are by the metaphors they use, she thought. Any minute now he'll say, "at this point in time." If it's not metaphors then it's adjectives. Adjectives are the curse of America. Yesterday a paper reviewed Cris Williamson's new album saying, "a sensual full-blooded haunting voice. Ms. Williamson sets the inside of your cool head reverberating with perfectly controlled hot sound. A four star winner." Christ, why didn't he just say, "She's great." I thought getting paid by the word went out with Dickens. People are always describing, modifying, qualifying. It's that or parroting commercials: Try it, you'll like it. I can't believe I ate the whole thing. How's your love life? Tv is the chewing gum of the mind or did Fred Allen say "eye?" Sometimes I think my friends in the thirteenth century were better off. They never suffered the disillusionment of a Toni home permanent run amuk. For them a spade was a spade; they didn't call it a delving instrument. What's happened? Why can't people take what is anymore? Do they have to verbalize a person or thing before they can believe it's real? Assbackwards. It's all assbackwards. Hang the soul who wrote, "In the beginning was the Word." He cost us untainted experience.

" . . . and I trust we'll all put our best foot forward." Fred finished. Speaking for thirty minutes exhilarated Fred and he was patting everyone within reach on the back, slugging away the scotch, and laughing much too loud.

Marcia Gahagan, the only other woman in the department, came over to Carole. "I see you survived the long, hot summer."

"It wasn't as bad as I thought it would be. How was Paris?"

"Exquisite as always if you ignore the people themselves. I never tire of the museums. I made a fascinating side trip to East Berlin. The museum there is quite good—superb actually—but how drab the city is. The difference between East Berlin and West Berlin is the difference between night and day. I don't think the Russians will ever let the Germans forget, you know?"

"And the Americans forgive everything if the offending nation buys a coca cola franchise," Carole replied.

Marcia started to say something in return but Fred, who had been inching his way over, achieved his goal at last, draping a boss's arm around both female employees.

"Marcia, Carole and I held down the fort this summer."

Marcia couldn't pointedly ignore him; she was coming up for tenure. "That must have made it a pleasant summer, Fred. I know how highly you regard Carole's work. Do excuse me, I've got to run up to the Lycee to pick up Michele."

Fred got chummy. "Mind if I ask you a personal question, Carole?" And before she could refuse, he babbled, "How's your love life?"

"Fantastic." She turned on her heel and left. Carole was tenured seven years ago.

Ilse kissed the oblique muscle twisting down into Carole's crotch. She draped her hair over Carole's thighs keeping her lips busy around the lower abdomen. Ilse loved to torment Carole. Through the older woman she had learned the pleasures of restraint. Slowly she would turn Carole into an ocean of hot tides. The power of her own sexuality made her heady. She used to think of her clitoris as a red acorn but now she thought of herself as a sea anemone. She could no longer localize her centers of pleasure: Carole synthesized her body. She had her first multiple orgasm with Carole and she loved her for that.

That time they were leaning up against the pillows, Carole drinking a coke as usual. She stored ice cubes in her mouth and kissed Ilse's whole body. When Carole buried her lips between Ilse's open legs, she lost the boundaries of her conventional self. Maybe it was the shock of ice on steam heat but Ilse didn't know where she left off and Carole began. Once you know how, it's easy, she flashed. She was learning to slip in and out of physical peaks at will. She felt a tremendous bond to Carole. Lying on top of her, she feared their rib cages would lock. Their thigh bones would merge. They'd have to learn to walk all over again. She pulled her fingernails along the older woman's sides, then slid her arms under Carole's shoulders and cradled the back of her head. With mounting force Carole moved further and further into Ilse's own body. The pounding vein between the inside of the thigh and the crotch beat underneath Ilse's clitoris. With her face nestled in the tall woman's neck she felt the same racing heartbeat under her lips. Held by the small of the back she felt motionless and weightless. When Carole groaned, "Now, Ilse, now," she felt that she had ridden out a tidal wave. The rocking motion and the burning vein directly underneath her brought forth a gush and a shudder. Ilse cried. She didn't know why. Coming together like that made her cry. Her mind pushed words away and the tears rolled along her nose into her mouth. Carole engulfed her with affection, kissed her, licking the salt. Stroking Ilse's hair Carole felt protective. She knew Ilse could take care of herself but for that vulnerable moment she shielded the woman facing the test of fragility, shared fragility. She let Ilse break the moment whenever she was ready.

"Do you know Pussblossom didn't budge the whole time we were making love?"

Pussblossom opened her eyes to a slit. She was on her back, front paws curled, hind legs sprawled, her short, fluffy tail lying motionless between her legs. She looked like a courtesan.

Carole ran her finger along the silver cheek. "Blossom, have you no shame?"

The cat turned her head, closed her eyes, and purred.

"How was Freddie Fowler today?"

"A pompous ass, as usual. Did you survive your meeting or did Olive stay away?"

"She was there all right. She went into a tirade about how I'm leading the group and leaders are elitist and I shouldn't do so much work. Hardly anyone listens to her any more but she's shrewd enough to single out the issues that sidetrack people. So we spent the whole fucking meeting discussing whether I was a leader or not and what did that mean. There's a thin line between collectivity and chaos, you know, and people like Olive are always stepping over it."

"From an outsider's point of view, a political group without leadership is committing suicide."

"A year ago I wouldn't have agreed with you but now I'm beginning to see not all people define responsibility the same way and things don't get done unless a few people take up the slack responsibility, sort of pick up what the others have left behind. Does that make sense to you?"

"Sure it makes sense to me. But don't you think leadership is more than completing projects? I like to think of it as a vision, or as a talent. Some people sing and some people don't. So some people have a political talent and some don't. I don't know how you tolerate people who try to tear you down when you're working for them, for all of us, really."

"That's what hurts the most. I expect men to treat me like shit but I sure as hell never expected it from other women." Carole started to say something but Ilse quickly added, "But I know why they do it. It's woman-hatred, you know? I mean they hate themselves so much they couldn't possibly respect another woman. Equality for those people means every other woman has to be as miserable as she is. Scares me, really fucking scares me. Here I am working my ass off and I'm not running the group or giving orders and this woman calls me an elitist. And even if everyone else by now knows she's vicious there are lots of others like her in the world."

"How people misuse your work isn't your responsibility, Ilse. No matter what you do someone can always twist it and use it against you. The hell with them. Keep doing what you can do."

"Yeah, but it hurts."

"Where did you ever get the idea things were going to be easy? Maybe what hurts is that people don't like you. Like I said, the hell with them. You can't live for other people. Look at what messes they make of their lives. You'd allow opinion to sway you? Never."

"But the whole point of the movement is to make women responsible to each other, to put each other first instead of giving our energies to men. I can't disregard other women like that."

"Until you put yourself first you're a liar. You'll try to get your way under the table without being aware of it and that will really destroy your women's movement. If all you people would sit down and figure out what you need in your lives, you'd probably find you have a real basis for bonding. Idealism isn't going to get you anywhere. You hear me?"

"Carole, you sounded so Southern then. Where'd that accent come from?"

"Did I? A remnant of my childhood, I guess. Sometimes when something's close to the bone I fall into it."

"But why did you change the way you talk?"

"You try living in the North with a Southern accent and see how far you get. People make incredible assumptions about you."

"You just contradicted yourself. You know that? You got finished telling me not to be influenced by other people's opinions and here you changed something yourself."

"Goddammit, don't nit-pick. I was eighteen years old when I migrated up here to go to Vassar. I didn't know as much then and I was influenced. I wouldn't do it today but I'd like you to know for your information, that Yankees, once they hear a drawl, no longer take seriously anything the person says. Hell's fire."

"You know, that's one of the few things you've ever told me about yourself, about your past. Tell me other things."

"I was born November 28, 1932, just outside of Winchester, Virginia."

"I thought you were raised in Richmond."

"I was but the family had gone up to my grandmother's farm for Thanksgiving and Mother wanted to be with her mother when she had me. I spent all my summers there until I went to college, then I worked in the summers and hated every minute of it."

"Do you have brothers and sisters?"

"I have a brother, living, and a sister who died in 1958."

"More. I want to know when you came out. We're just getting to the good parts."

"Muffy Cadwalder. God, I haven't thought of her in years. Muffy and I were in the same class at Vassar. We both lived in Jewett."

"I was in Cushing," Ilse interrupted.

"There isn't much to tell about my flaming romance with Muffy . . . except that I fell in love with her in the hospital."

"Were you sick?" Ilse had her legs crossed and was all interest.

"No. Muff had a slip up. She was quite pregnant. In those days that was a fate worse than death, my dear, to be unmarried and pregnant. She came from a wealthy Chicago family and they had connections, obviously. She was also lucky enough to have an understanding mother who arranged the whole thing. Muff was terrified and asked me to go home with her for the weekend. She paid my way. Her mother and I stood out in the hallway and after the anesthetic they wheeled her down the hall into the operating room. As she rolled by she was singing at the top of her lungs: 'He was my man but he done me wrong.' At that precise moment I knew I was in love with fertile Muffy Cadwalder."

"Will you get to how you got her in bed!"

"Oh. Well, we went back to school together and the friendship stayed nonphysical for the next month but Muff and I were inseparable. I suppose since I

90

knew her darkest secret she felt that much closer to me. 'Frankenstein' was playing on campus, the old thirties' version, and we went to see it. After that she said she was afraid to sleep alone and could she sleep with me. There we were side by side in those damn little beds. I couldn't move. I lay there barely breathing, my heart pounding. I felt like all those old terrible cliches. So Muffy turns over to me on her side and starts talking about what dear friends we were and how she loved me. I kissed her. That may have been the bravest moment of my entire life."

"What'd she do?"

"She kissed me back."

"You are so difficult. What did you do then? I mean did you go down on her or inside of her or what?"

"Ilse! No, I didn't do any of those things our first time out. Neither of us was too certain of the mechanics of all this so we fumbled around a lot but it was a beginning."

"What broke you up?"

"After graduation I went to graduate school and she went off to Europe dressed in all the latest fashions, naturally."

"You always leave out your emotions. How did you feel?"

"Did it ever occur to you that someone may not want to wear her heart on her sleeve? My emotions and my emotional development are my business. I'm not sure you understand that. Your generation has been hopelessly corrupted by psychology."

"What are you getting so defensive for?"

"See: defensive. What kind of word is that? Are we

at a football game?"

"All right. Obstinate. Reserved. Aloof? How's that? So now tell me. That was some twenty-five years ago."

"Jesus, but you're persistent. My work was more important to me than playing house with Muffy Cadwalder. Yes, I was depressed but I never seriously thought I'd settle down with Muffy or marry her or whatever the hell you want to call it. I loved her but I wasn't ready to alter my life for her."

"What do you mean when you say 'settle down' or 'marry?'"

"I knew that was coming. I mean make a life together."

"And be monogamous?" Ilse's eyebrows almost touched her scalp.

"It was 1951. Everybody was monogamous. We didn't know anything else existed."

"Are you monogamous now?"

"What is this, twenty questions? I haven't thought about it. I suspect in my heart of hearts, to coin a phrase, I'm monogamous but that's me. Someone else is another way and don't try to get me off on a discussion of the politics of monogamy."

Ilse giggled. "Okay, okay, monogamy isn't exactly a burning issue to me, really. A lot of people get excited about it though." She raised her hand after a pause. Carole broke out laughing and put it down.

"Teacher," Ilse asked, "one more question?"

"Shoot."

"The piano player."

"Two of you," Carole threw up her hands in mock resignation. "Now you're getting as bad as Adele."

92

"That's my question. When did you meet Adele?"

"Graduate school. We were the only women there and we used to go out for coffee to talk. I knew it was the beginning of a beautiful friendship when she told me about her Catholic girlhood. Her huge rebellion was to call the Blessed Mother, Divurgent Mary. I was a Catholic too and my big moment was to whip through my beads mumbling, 'Hail Mary full of grace slipped on the floor and fell flat on her face.' We've been dear friends ever since."

"Adele's a Catholic?"

"Was. Why, did you think she was a Baptist or a Holy Roller?"

"Well, you never mention Adele's Blackness. How come?"

"What's to mention? All you have to do is look at her."

"Carole, that's not what I mean and you know it. When you two became friends, white and Black women weren't seen together."

"People probably thought she was my maid." Carole roared.

Ilse, at a complete loss because she couldn't fathom how anyone could laugh about race, sputtered, "Be serious. You had to be aware that you were breaking a code."

"Who put a poker up your ass? Yes people would look at us sometimes and yes if we went to 'The Half Note' or 'Jazz Gallery' we'd have to call up ahead of time and tell them so they'd put us in a corner in the back. But we went with men. She'd go with Richard Benton, a Black fellow, and I'd go with David, whose last name I forget. Anyway, David was white. In those days you didn't go anywhere without a man unless it was to a gay bar. And we dressed to kill. Bras with stays and underpants that came to the waist, panty girdles with clips. How did we move? And the shoes. Shoes changed every year. You could always tell the day trippers because they wore white shoes. When I think back on it, it was horrendous."

"You're off the track."

"Adele in the old days. So we got some dirty looks. We'd have gotten a lot more if we'd been a woman and a man."

"Coming from the South and all weren't you nervous about having a Black friend?"

"Ilse, show me a Yankee who wouldn't have been a little jumpy back then. Of course we knew we were crossing the line but we loved each other. I don't know, we clicked. We're meant to be best friends. BonBon would say we knew each other in another life. Hell. And we certainly never sat around and talked seriously about race."

"And you never went to bed with her?"

"I told you before, no."

"Maybe you didn't go to bed with her because she's Black."

"If that's the reason I never knew about it. I didn't go to bed with her because she was going with someone when I met her. God, but you're nosy."

"Yeah, but that marriage as you call it didn't last forever."

"Adele gets into long things. She lived with a woman named Carmen for twelve years. Adele doesn't fool around. By the time she broke up with Carmen I was with someone. Then when we broke up Adele was already with LaVerne. Besides, when you're friends with someone for that long you don't think of them that way."

"Not me. My friends are the people I sleep with."

"That's you," Carole said.

"You never told me you lived with anyone."

"Ilse, I am not going into another long story from my past. When I was twenty-eight I settled down with a person I'd like to forget—Rebecca Delaney. We lived together for six years and then we separated. Actually, I shouldn't say I'd like to forget her. One was as bad as the other there toward the end. Now roll over and go to sleep."

"Whose turn is it to be on the outside, yours or mine?"

"I forget."

"Good, then you hold me."

Carole curled up behind her, put her left arm underneath Ilse's pillow and dropped her right arm over her smooth side.

"Does Freddie Fowler know you're gay?"

"You're supposed to be asleep."

"Tell me then I promise, cross my heart and hope to die, that I'll go to sleep."

"Those women who are anti-leadership are making a big mistake with you. You can wear down any opposition you're so damned persistent. They ought to shove you right out in front." Carole sighed. "Fred Fowler may very well know I'm gay but you can hardly think I'm going to sit down in his office and discuss it with him."

"We all have to come out so they know how many we are and how we are just real, you know. No one can be in the closet because it hurts all of us."

"We've been over this before. I've read the articles on the subject, I understand the logic of it, but what are you going to do with all the people who lose their jobs, especially the people with children?"

"That's the point. If we all come out we can't lose our jobs; there are too many of us."

"Shut up and go to sleep. I have to teach tomorrow. Want me to walk into class with a lesbian purple star on?"

"Yes."

"Let's go to sleep. Anyway, I'm not dead yet. I might come out but I'll do it when I'm good and goddamn ready. Good night!"

"Night."


Rounding the corner onto Lexington Avenue, Adele stopped to get a hot dog from the Sabrett vendor. The orange and blue umbrella wavered every time a car went by but the man ignored them, jabbing at the hot dogs as though they were escaping eels.

"Lots of mustard, please."

Armed with a bright yellow hot dog Adele spun through the doors to Bloomingdale's and began the fight for the elevators. Whatever the hour the department store hosted two compatible, parasitic factions: upper East Side housewives and troops of faggots deeply devoted to gaudy consumerism. When Adele first moved to New York City, a polite, well bred young woman accustomed to decent manners, she found herself crushed in the crowds. Navigating Bloomie's and its cruisy clientele then would have unraveled her to the breakdown point. Year after year of being pounded on the relentless anvil of the city taught the outwardly refined woman a survival lesson. Instead of weaving through shoppers saying, "Excuse me, please," she thrust her dripping hot dog in front of her and said in her best Bronx accent, "Watch out, watch out, ya wanna get mustard all over ya?" People parted like the Red Sea. Brandishing her hot dog on the elevator insured no one would crowd into her and if they did it was their cleaning bill. The doors opened on LaVerne's floor and Adele grandly stepped off oblivious to the raised eyebrows behind her. A small boy and his mother were waiting for the down elevator.

"Here, kid, gorge yourself."

The mother snatched the hot dog out of her son's hand, no doubt because Adele was Black; after all you never could tell if those people's hands were clean. She stomped over to the ashtray between the elevators and dumped the hot dog in the sand amid the crushed cigarette butts. The boy, outraged, snatched it back, defiantly tearing off the end with his snarling little mouth. Adele could hear them bickering on her way back to LaVerne.

Disrupting authority, any form of authority, was one of Adele's delights. Being a wise woman she sped away from the scene of unrest she created. For some reason a picture of Ilse registered in her mind.

I ought to give that woman a lesson. Ilse's got to learn there's more than one way to skin a cat. Adele laughed to herself. If you can't beat 'em, cheat 'em.

LaVerne was bending over to pick up her purse when Adele caught sight of her.

"M-m-m, m-m-m, I'd know that ass anywhere."

LaVerne jumped up as though someone shot her. "Will you behave yourself? You want to get me fired from here, woman?"

"I'd like to get you fired up."

"Come on, hot pants, let's get out of here before it's too late." LaVerne seized her elbow then let go. "See, you make me forget where I am."

"Honey, I had such a good time with my hot dog today. When I got off the elevator I gave it to a little white boy standing there with his mother and did they start in on each other. She pulled it out of his hand and put it in the dirty old ashtray. He ran over and took it back. Kinda warms your heart, such a touching family scene."

"I'm beginning to think you don't like children."

"That's a terrible lie. I love children especially if they're well done."

"Damn, all these years we've been together and I still don't know what's going to come flying out of your mouth. I bet you're the only person in New York City who has to have her mouth inspected by the Sanitation Department."

Adele laughed. "Not me, darling, that honor belongs to Che Che LaWanga who rents a subway stall from the transit authority."

"Che Che LaWanga?"

"You never met the bread basket? A hot lunch for orphans, take off your pants, boys, Betsy Ross's flag is flying."

"What on earth are you singing about?"

"*Hello Dolly*. Che Che LaWanga was a drag queen stripper friend of BonBon's and Creampuff's. He used to have a glory hole down in the tubes. We'd sing that song to him every time we saw him."

"That's disgusting. Men are perverse. Doesn't matter if they're straight or if they're gay they are sick out of their minds when it comes to sex."

"What's it to you? You're not fucking any of them."

"That's true. Any news from Bon?"

"Carole heard from her today. Creampuff gave her a watch engraved, 'I'm with you every second.' They always celebrate the day they met. Don't you love it?"

"That's almost as tacky as last year when she gave her an ankle bracelet inscribed 'Heaven's Above.' " LaVerne sighed. "To each his own."

"Her own, Ilse may be lurking about, her own," Adele corrected.

"Since you're taking me out to dinner tonight, tell me where we're going and then tell me what is going on with Carole and Ilse."

"Thought we'd go to Catch of the Sea. You feel like some sea food? We'll be close to home and we can walk back."

"Ah, it's so nice out let's walk up to the place. It'll take fifteen or twenty minutes depending on whether we get lost window shopping."

"I left my track shoes at home."

"Your feet bothering you? Come on then, we'll take a cab," urged LaVerne.

"Nah, I don't walk enough anyway. That's how Carole keeps in great shape. She walks everywhere."

"She was a beautiful woman in her day. God knows, she's still good to look at. When I saw those old pictures you have of the two of you in graduate school, well, she took my breath away. She looks like Carole Lombard."

"Yeah, but I got your heart."

"Adele, you got it all," LaVerne laughed at her;

A warm woman, LaVerne lacked the career drive of her lover and of Carole. She enjoyed her work and she worked hard. She possessed a flair for color, for clothes, for sensing trends, but she wasn't involved in her work the way they were absorbed by what they did. She had no pretensions that what she did was useful but at least it wasn't boring. Her own pleasing looks and diplomatic approach to the business guaranteed advancement. She knew she'd be moved upstairs probably this year and they'd flash her around to show they were an equal opportunity employer, and kill two birds with one stone, race and sex. But hell, she thought, it's better than being left out. Besides, they'll give me that long vacation so I can go with Dell to the Yucatan. LaVerne wasn't the intellectual that Adele was but she was smart and she had a gift for living, a gift for opening herself up to people and the new ideas they brought with them. Adele loved that in her.

"So, what's happening with Carole?" LaVerne asked again.

"She's up because she finished her paper. The thing with Ilse stays about the same. They fence a lot."

"I guess that's inevitable. Even if Ilse weren't so heavy into the women's movement the age gap is bound to produce tensions."

"I reminded her again of September twenty-ninth. It's driving her crazy."

"You two are such know-it-alls. If one has a surprise the other one gets ulcers trying to figure it out. Actually, sometimes I think you're twins, two peas in a pod."

"Honey, we'd have made medical history." Adele paused and caught LaVerne by the sleeve. "Wait a sec, I want to look in this window. Aren't those Folon prints unique?"

"I like the colors and the strange people. Dell, you think Carole is riding for a fall?"

They walked half a block before Adele answered. "I do but something tells me it's going to be good for her. Pain isn't always the enemy."

"That's the beautiful truth. What is it that Carole says about lovers? You know, that famous line of hers?"

"Oh, we betray ourselves by the lovers we choose." Adele smiled at LaVerne. "That means we lucked out, my love."

"Even our fights are fun. I like to think we don't actually fight, we creatively disagree."

"My dear."

"What do you think Ilse says about Carole?"

"Carole's a complex woman. It isn't as though she can't attract people, most anyone she wants, really, so there's something in Ilse. I know they're in flames every time they see one another but that can't be all. I think it has something to do with Ilse's forwardness. She's bold and she challenges Carole all the time with those ideas of social change she's got. I like Ilse even though she suffers from the arrogance of youth. She's learned a lot from books. Now she's got to humble herself and learn from people."

"Oh well, I was that way. I thought I knew everything at twenty-one." LaVerne dropped her voice. "It's a big jump from smart to motherwit."

"Amen."

"Honey, do you think Carole's trying to recapture youth or something? She is more than twenty years older than Ilse."

"No, I really don't. She knows she's old enough to be her mother. But Carole doesn't think that way. She never makes jokes about getting old or drags it into conversation. I think she's one of the few people I know who's made a graceful concession to the elements."

"Something I think I'd better do. I'm getting closer and closer to forty."

"LaVerne, you know I think all this age business is silliness. Can't hold back the years and who wants to? What's more boring than innocence? Anyway, the years aren't as important as how you've used them. It's like the parable about the talents. 'Your years are your wealth.' "

"Bible School. I had to memorize every one of those damn parables by heart. Let me tell you how I used to wish Jesus had been born deaf and dumb."

"The story that made a doubter out of me was the one where he's up there feeding everyone from bits of fish and loaves of bread. Even at seven I knew that was an outright lie. If I'd told a story like that at home Momma would have slapped my face and here some nun is telling me it's God's honest truth," Adele mused.

"How'd we get on Jesus's case anyway?"

"I forget. Wait, you were moaning about getting gray and I said getting old is like the dude who left

102

the three men money, remember, and the dumb man buries the money."

"That's what I like about us, we never take the direct route. Now tell me more about Ilse. You didn't finish that off."

"Oh. Well, I think Ilse is in some way connected to Carole's background. Ilse comes from money as you know. Carole has always been fascinated and repelled by people who had it easy. Here is this Boston rich kid repudiating her own past and calling it a revolution. A potent combination for Ms. Hanratty."

"You come from money. I don't sense any lurking hostility from Carole toward you."

"That's because I'm Black. It's a mark, a proof of injustice, of suffering. We're equals in her eyes because I haven't had it all given to me. Carole despises people who've had it handed to them and do nothing with it. She only respects people who work. I guess that includes working to remove the stigma of inherited wealth. She's a strange combination of Spartan and aesthete."

"I never thought of her that way but now that you've said it I can see where someone like Ilse would draw her. Ilse's got it all handed to her and she's handing it all back. That takes a certain amount of courage."

"Yes and no. The reason why I could never get into the peace movement was because most of those folk wanted moral points for giving back the money, for bucking the system. They protested as much out of ego as out of ruffled justice. Don't trust that. Besides, who's to say they can't go back and get the money if they change their mind, if the going turns ugly? You know that old biographical stage direction: Enter left. Exit right."

"You never did."

Startled, Adele hesitated. "I . . . no, I didn't, but that was different. I wasn't marching against the government—marching for civil rights. My daddy wanted me to be a lawyer like himself and I wanted to study art. I have to give credit to Dad. He paid my way through undergraduate school. When I left I didn't take any more from him. That's not exactly repudiating him. I went to graduate school on my own. Things were cool on the home front for years after that, but Dad hasn't cut me out of his will or anything drastic."

"He'll probably leave you only his law books out of spite, just wait."

"Hells bells, as Lester would say. And if he did I'd manage. Got this far on my own."

LaVerne announced, "And we got this far together. Are you hungry after all that exercise?"

They took a table by the window in the white and blue restaurant. After the waitress brought them drinks Adele lifted her glass to LaVerne and whispered, "I love you."

Across the courtyard Lucia, in a mother earth mood, was baking fresh bread. The smell of it invaded Ilse's small cottage. Vito chased a busy fly and Ilse was curled up in her bed reading Mao's remarks on art at the Yenan conference. Mao continually surprised her. He was so practical. Carole's insistence that art was the morning star of revolution prompted her to look at what others had to say on the subject. Initially she thought Carole was firing another flashy line but grudgingly she was losing some of her distrust of the beautiful.

She had feared beauty, feared anyone consecrated by creativity. Mother forced the so-called fine arts down her throat until she thought she'd choke. At school she was expected to flutter over Beethoven or swoon at Renoir. She hated the whole thing. Gaining a feminist viewpoint taught her that art was nothing but an extended commercial for the rich. They celebrated their values or lack of them, their petty morality or latest conquest. And so she threw the baby out with the bathwater. She forgot about Mark Twain. She didn't know about the artisans of the Middle Ages. She'd never even heard of Muriel Spark, Bertha Harris, Gwendolyn Brooks, Tillie Olsen, Barbara Deming, Maya Angelou, and all the other women fighting their way into recognition. She thought of art the way she thought of tennis. It was for the white and the rich. Worse than tennis it was almost all men.

As Ilse never faltered in her feminist faith so Carole never faltered in her faith that humans must create beauty or spiritually die. Carole forced Ilse to reconsider what she had thought was a dead issue. She still didn't think of art the way Carole did but she reconsidered it from a political standpoint. Could art be useful? Can it teach? Can it activate people?

Why am I afraid of beauty? All my life I've been told I was beautiful. It was as though I was an art object, admired, prized, handled, and, later, polished. Mother saw to that. Daddy was too busy making money to participate in my growing up although he did manage to tell me I looked pretty. He also managed to look at my report cards. I hate them both. They're self-deceived, cowardly, and inflexible. They are the enemy. Really, my parents are the enemy. Even Mother. I can understand why she did everything she did but I can't forgive her for it. Even if she had no choice then she has a choice now. My mother should be right here in the movement beside me instead of taking ups in Brookline. Maybe that's why I fear beauty or art or whatever it is that Carole pursues. It might get me off course, drag me back into my proper past. I don't want a past. I want to start new. I want to be reborn. Reborn. That's why I'm having trouble talking to Carole about feminism. I'm changed. I'm not what I was or what I was raised to be. I'm not what any woman was raised to be. I'm a new world. I haven't even got a language yet for what's happened to me. None of us have. Perhaps we do need artists to develop that language. I never thought of it that way.

The phone rang. It was Alice Reardon reminding Ilse that tonight's meeting was changed from her house to Harriet's over on East Sixth Street.

Hurrying by Cooper Union, Ilse took a right under the scaffolding and ran smack into the local, neighborhood exhibitionist waving his prick like a pink handkerchief and breathing as though he needed an iron lung. Ilse slacked her pace, faced him directly, and said in the sweetest voice possible, "That looks like a penis only smaller." She then crossed Third Avenue at a brisk pace arriving at Harriet's apartment right on time.

Olive, glowering on the floor, spat, "Everybody's

here so let's start. We've wasted enough time already."

Ilse almost said she'd been on time but figured why bother.

Olive continued, "I've been approached by the *Village Rag*. They say they want to do a piece on us. Maybe one of us could even write it although those details would have to be worked out later. So I think we ought to talk about it."

Alice replied, "What we ought to talk about is media policy. We've been so busy with projects and meetings about meetings that we don't have a guideline for things like this."

"What do we need a policy for? Why can't we just decide about the *Rag*? If we start in on a policy we'll be here all night and I don't want to go out on the East Village streets late." Sue pouted.

Suella Matson was one of Olive's last remaining devotees. She had changed her name to Sue Betsychild and let the hair on her chin grow into a healthy stubble. Somehow that seemed contradictory to Ilse but she knew better than to bring it to Sue's attention.

Olive's other remaining troop member was Ann Rappaport who changed her name to Annie Amazon. Even in blazing weather, five foot one inch Annie wouldn't be seen without her black leather jacket sparkling with silver studs. She backed up Sue's statement with a gusty, "Yeah." Ilse couldn't imagine that Annie Amazon was afraid to walk the streets at night. *Yeah* what? she thought. *Yeah* she's afraid to walk the streets or *yeah* we don't need to get into a media policy?

"Trying to figure out a way to handle the establishment media might take longer than one meeting," Ilse offered, "but we should do it. Otherwise we're going to deal with the problem piecemeal and we'll screw ourselves up. Today it's the *Village Rag*, three months later it'll be *Esquire*. We need some criteria to measure this by."

Sue Betsychild growled, "They need an answer by this Thursday.

Ilse was bored and angry with the constant hassles. "They might not get their answer this Thursday. I think the direction of this group is more important than pleasing some editor at the *Rag*."

Olive exploded. "Shut up, James. We don't need you telling us what to do."

Harriet tried to calm things down. "Don't personalize an issue, Olive. We do need to develop some policy for the group where the press is concerned. If we don't, we run the risk of making serious mistakes."

"What kind of mistakes?" Annie baited her taking a deep drag out of a crooked little cigar.

Brenda Zellner inserted her level mind into the argument, "Look how the press misrepresented the Panthers to the public. And look how the press jerked off at the protests over the Miss America Pageant. The establishment media has never shown itself hospitable to political groups that could rock it's own interests and we're one of those groups."

"Whadda ya mean, Panthers? And how are we shaking up the *Rag*? This is ridiculous. We could use coverage," Olive fired back.

"Olive, why don't you check out the *Rag's* masthead? Check out its advertising? How many women do you see on the board or on the staff? H-m-m? The media is run by white, middle- to upper-middle-class men and they don't want to hear from women's liberation much less organized lesbians unless they can make some money out of us. Get serious. They'll try to make us look like a bunch of crazies," Brenda answered.

Alice whispered in Ilse's ear. "Unfortunately we have a few crazies. Maybe we could give them Olive and they'd keep her as Exhibit A."

Ilse had to stifle a guffaw. Alice was her closest friend in their political circles. Attractive in a quiet way, the movement saved Alice from becoming a parson's wife but she brought the same steely patience of a missionary to the group. Alice had no illusions that organizing was glamorous. At twenty-five she realized that work is its own reward and no one ever has a handle on the future. All you can do is keep your shoulder to the wheel.

"If we had a write-up we'd get more members," Annie bitched.

"We don't need new members," Ilse said.

"Oh sure, if new people come in then you can't control the group," Olive accused.

"Fuck off, Olive. Numbers aren't important right now. It's more important for us to have some clarity, some understanding among ourselves first. Then if we want to build a large organization we can. If we open the doors now it will destroy all that we've done so far."

"That's unsisterly," Sue hurled at her.

Even Alice was getting fed up. "Bullshit. We're not a social group. We do need to decide where we're going before we take in new people."

"I think we're getting off the subject. The subject is a media policy," Harriet stated.

"Then I say we ought to take advantage of the contradictions and use the *Rag* to our own advantage," Olive pressed, furious.

"You have no control over what gets in that paper. They can let you edit the article, then put back in whatever they want, and give you a song and dance afterwards. Christ, how can you trust these people? How can anyone trust the press?" Brenda expounded.

"They exposed Watergate," Ann said.

"Watergate isn't the women's movement or lesbians. Watergate is still in their realm of experience. It offends their convenient morality but it's safe inside their frame of reference. We are completely beyond their ability to understand us. We're new women. New people. They're blind to us. We'd be fools to allow ourselves to be used by these people for copy. Do you think they care about our analysis? Hell no. We'd make fantastic copy for them. The article would say how sexually desirable or undesirable we are. Whether we looked like men. Who is sleeping with whom. Do we like men? Do we hate men? That's what they want to know. They're unable to hear the questions we're asking." Ilse waxed hot.

Harriet supported her. "Right on. If we do ever use the establishment media then it's got to be on our terms. That's why we need a media policy. Right now exposure is too dangerous and could hurt us. We're still too unformed. If we were a reformist group trying to pass legislation or awareness of oppression then the press would have its uses immediately. But we're not. We're revolutionaries. Or radicals. I don't know.

110

None of those words seem to apply. They're old-fashioned . . ."

"We know what you mean," Brenda encouraged.

"Well, I mean our purpose isn't to put a band-aid on a gaping wound. Our answer is economic—it isn't just abortion or no discrimination against lesbians. We have more to us than that and we need to tie those ideas together and to develop a thorough program. The press is irrelevant to us now."

"America lives by the media! How will we ever reach the masses?" Olive bordered on the hysterical now.

"I don't think there are any masses." Alice spoke firmly. "There are millions of individuals but no masses. I refuse to categorize people. That's what male supremacy teaches us, to fit people into nifty little categories that destroy them. There are no masses and we degrade ourselves and the people we want to reach by going through a press, a medium, that conceives of them as a mass."

"You're quibbling. Coverage is coverage. How are people going to know about us and what we stand for if we don't use tv and stuff like that?" Sue at this point was more perplexed than angry.

"By our work." Alice went on, "By our own network of communication. Do you think people trust television? It shows them a body count in one minute followed by a Geritol commercial in the next minute."

"Shit. People are stupid. They'll believe what's on tv." Olive ridiculed her.

Ilse rose to her feet. The months of enduring Olive had taken their toll. Her temper flew out the window.

"People are stupid. If you think people are stupid then why are you in this group? Why do you even bother with the movement? What makes you so much better than anyone else? And who is going to listen to you or any of us if we look down on the people we're trying to talk to? Nixon operated on the premise that people are stupid. Do you want to operate that way? You have no respect for anyone because you don't respect yourself. Why don't you take your hang-ups and just get the hell out of here!"

Olive charged over to Ilse and took a swing at her. Annie and Sue trailed right behind her. Alice, Harriet, and Brenda formed a wall between them and Ilse.

"Sit down, sit down and cool off, goddammit," Harriet yelled.

Olive collapsed in a lump and began her famous crying routine. Annie mothered her and the chains on her jacket and pants almost rattled out Olive's sobs. The other women, not ready for such a sulphurous reaction, sat in stunned silence.

Alice finally spoke. "I think the needs of this group and your needs aren't the same, Olive. I can't speak for anyone else but as far as I'm concerned I can't work with you."

It hadn't dawned on Olive that she might be thrown out. If she felt sorrowful she covered it in another outburst. "Elitist snobs. You all suck up to Ilse. You talk about ideology. S'all crap. We're supposed to love each other."

"No," Ilse stepped in. "We're supposed to pull our weight. It's unrealistic to expect we'll all love each other. The most we can ask for is to respect each other and to work for a common goal. If we're going to love each other it'll come out of working side by side not because somebody put it down on paper."

"Well, I'm going to go to the *Rag* and give them a real article. And anyone who wants to can get away from these pigs and join me."

Sue Betsychild and Annie Amazon followed her out the door. Annie snuck a look back to see if anyone was coming but no one budged. They heard Annie's chains jingling all the way to the front door.

"What decayed ego structures those people must have, like rotting persimmons." Brenda shook her head.

"That's poetic, Brendie." Alice put her arm around her.

"This had to happen sometime. If we're going to talk about this group and its direction we ought to examine why we let this drag on so long. That may not be our first priority of discussion but why are women such setups for emotions? Damn." Harriet sat back down again shaking her head.

"Because we're the peacemakers, the ones responsible for soothing ruffled feathers," Brenda said.

"Partly, but I also think it's because we're unsure of ourselves." The women stared at Ilse. "We're trying to pull an ideology together; we've got a lot of it but we're shaky in parts. We haven't been in political struggle that long. We're not taken seriously so that doesn't help one bit. And look at us. Look how young we are—we're still getting our own lives together. It's pretty easy for someone to run us around, you know, especially with tears. Christ, if there's one thing women respond to it's tears."

"Ilse, you wouldn't by any chance be saying we

113

should be unemotional, pseudo-rational, shut off emotions the way men do, would you?" Harriet questioned her in an even tone.

"I don't know, Harriet. Remember when we first formed this group and people talked about getting in touch with their emotions? We thought if we could reach some emotional core that revolution would magically follow. I'm not saying we should shut off feelings or anything like that but more and more I'm favoring hard intellectual labor. We've had enough time organizing to sit down and figure out what went right and what went wrong. I know somewhere I'm beginning to doubt emotion. I mean we've all been raised in a system hostile to our needs, a system that thinks of us as functions not persons. How can we fully trust our responses, you know? For all we know compassion could be a conditioned response and one that continues to keep us oppressed by putting other people's troubles ahead of our own. Isn't that what good women always do, sacrifice? We could be making a virtue out of oppression."

"This still isn't media policy but it's fascinating," Brenda responded.

Alice followed, "I have the same questions, Ilse, questions that would have seemed dangerous to me even three months ago. But one thing still seems dangerous to me and that's withdrawing to do hard intellectual labor. I can't see how that won't just isolate us from others. We have to keep organizing and try to draw our conclusions at the same time."

"Yes and no," Ilse said. "We could have dances for the gay community for the next five years and I don't think we'd learn anything more by it. We've ex-

114

hausted it as a learning process. Other people who haven't been around the movement as long as we have could take it over and learn from it the same way we did. I mean there's got to be some organized chain of experience. Here we've learned something. Now if we sit down and write it out that's fine. Women in Wisconsin can read and learn. Women in New York could also learn by performing that function we've begun and then move on when they've learned by doing. It's incredible how we haven't been able to transmit our knowledge—and one of the reasons is that we don't have large organizations to provide shared ways for people to learn. A position paper isn't enough. It's time to recognize that some of us know more by virtue of years in the movement and some by virtue of special skills."

"I hate the way that sounds." Brenda grinned. "But I know it's true. We always put the niceties of theory before the realities of practice. Time to get our feet back on the ground."

"I'm not sure we can make decisions yet. Do we have enough evidence?" Judy Avery—who'd been silent all evening—piped up.

Ilse turned to her. "All decisions are made on insufficient evidence."

"Yeah, but do we have the right to make decisions for other people?" Alice wanted to know.

"Alice, what other people? It's a question of responsibility. Parents have to make decisions for their children. You can't let an infant wander around. You make decisions when the child is fed, cleaned, exercised. That's responsibility—and hopefully you teach the child to be responsible for herself. Well, little girls who are now one year old will be affected by whether we make decisions or whether we default. And what about adults? Look at all the women who flood women's centers trying to find a way out of the maze. You know what we used to do with them? We'd throw them right in with us, in the thick of whatever program we were working on or whatever political battle we were fighting. What a fucked-up thing to do. That's like dumping someone who doesn't know how to swim in a river with a fast current. No wonder the attrition rate was so high. We've got to take responsibility for people who come to us. Where are they coming from? What do they want? Do they even know what they want? Can we help them? Can they help us? We have to develop an organization that various people can participate in according to their various needs, skills, desires, you know? We can't level everyone. And under the guise of sisterhood that's what we've been doing. Really, listen to me. We've acted on the assumption that everyone has to be a fulltime political person, an organizer, a theoretician. That's fucked. We've done to women what men have done to us. We've taken their identities away by expecting them all to perform the same functions."

"Give me time to sort this out, it's been an exhausting meeting. I want to go on with this when we're fresh. Now that the obstruction is off the road we can all search for the answers with more trust." Harriet sighed.

"Wait, before we break up for the night I want to read off three criteria I picked out of a pamphlet I read the other night. You might want to write them down and we can get to them at the next meeting or one by one," Alice called out. "This is to measure a program or an activity. Okay? Number one: Does it meet material and/or emotional needs? Number two: Does it bring women together? Teach us how to win? Number three: Does it weaken the current power structure? That's it."

Catching the bus on East Ninth Street, Alice and Ilse rode over to Hudson Street together.

"Ilse, isn't it funny how we can criticize each other face to face—and that's a breakthrough—but it's still hard to praise each other?"

"Never thought of it."

"I'd like to tell you to your face that I think you have a fine mind. Who knows if we'll find all the answers but you ask the deep questions, the questions that are underneath so many of our unconsidered actions or beliefs. I'm really glad we're together. Whenever women like Olive bum me out I remind myself if it weren't for the movement I'd never have met people like you."

Ilse held her hand, "Thank you. I—I'm glad you're here too."

"Maybe it's because I turned twenty-five last month, a quarter of a century. Sounds so old. I've been alive for that long? But I'm realizing this is a life's work, this movement. I will fight this fight for as long as I live. That hadn't dawned on me before. I feel a new seriousness. I feel that my life is measurable. I don't know if that makes sense but when I was in high school and even college I had a vague notion that my life was infinite. Thought I could paint and travel and sing and read and do anything. I don't feel that way anymore. My life is now definite and finite. I've chosen the thing I'm going to do and suddenly all the muddle cleared away. It's peaceful. Now there's a contradiction: here I've decided to spend my life fighting and it's given me peace."

"No, it sounds right. I know what you're saying. I don't think I have as clear a sense of my job yet as you do. I mean, I know I'll be in the movement for the rest of my life too but you're so talented. You could organize anything from building a battleship to a tea party on the White House lawn—for lesbians. You amaze me how you can pull people and materials together. I can organize but not as good as you."

"That's because you don't suffer fools gladly."

"Well, if you mean Olive, no."

"No. Olive is malignant. I mean you expect every one to be as intelligent as you are. You're not patient. When you work with people you have to accept their limitations as well as their gifts."

"Now I feel guilty."

"Don't feel guilty. Wasn't it you tonight who said we can't level people, we have to use our talents where they do the most good? So you're a fair organizer. There are better people than you at that. But you've got a fearless questioning mind. So think. Anyway, you don't have to make a decision on the bus."

"Better not. Here's our stop. I'll walk you home."

"Thanks. Hey, are you still seeing Carole?"

"Yeah, I was supposed to go up there tonight but the meeting ran so late. I forgot to call her too."

"Want to call from my place?"

"No thanks. I'm only two minutes away from you

118

anyway. I'll call her when I get home and give her a full report."

"I thought you said she wasn't interested in politics."

"Not the way we are. Like you said, I judged her by my standards but compared to other nonmovement people she's pretty aware."

"She's striking. If she went out speaking people would join the movement just to get to know her." Alice laughed.

"I'll have to tell her that."

"Sounds as though things are good between you."

"I guess. She pisses me off sometimes. I mean, I guess I do want her in the movement. Her attitude of being above it all bothers me but she does give me emotional support. Age makes a difference. Things that upset me don't phase her. Flat, you know? Her perspective is different. She's seen more, at least more of the everyday world."

"We need that. A lot of the older women are reformists which doesn't do us a hell of a lot of good."

"Yeah, I know. Too bad those older lesbians are still in that goddamned closet."

"You'd think they'd choke on the hangers by now." Alice laughed.

"Mind if I borrow that line?"

"Nah, what's mine is yours. Thanks for walking me home."


Ilse walked the short two blocks to her house. Worn by the meeting, she walked slower than usual even though she wanted to call Carole.

The narcotic media, it desensitizes people to violence. Why didn't I say that at the meeting? We're surrounded by crime, violence, and nostalgia. For some reason she couldn't discover, some lost connection, she remembered a conversation she had with Adele the last time the four of them were together. She wanted to know why Adele studied such cruel people as the Aztecs. Adele told her that she wasn't an Aztec scholar, her field was the classic age of the Maya, but she had a passing knowledge of Aztec life.

"Why do you think they were so cruel?" Adele asked her back.

"Because they practiced human sacrifice. Not just one a year but lots of sacrifice."

Adele answered her, "And you think we don't?"

What stood out in her mind was Adele's explanation about why they had such rituals. It wasn't that the Aztec gods were especially hateful. They were hungry. All life is hungry. The destruction of living things is the drum beat of life. Death fed life. If there wasn't constant death then the life of the gods grew weak and how can a culture stand when its gods die? They fed their gods and then they communed to take some of the gods' strength into themselves.

Vito's hungry meows erased the Aztecs from her mind. She fed the cat and called Carole.

"Hello."

"Hi, I'm sorry I didn't call earlier."

"Ilse, where are you?"

"I'm home. The meeting ran late and I'm wiped out. We finally had the blow-out with Olive. She wanted the *Village Rag* to do an article on us. Can you imagine?"

"Sure," Carole said. "They could title it, 'Orphans

120

of the Norm.' "

"Jesus christ, Carole, after tonight that's not funny. She was screeching at me that I'm an elitist and why do we need a media policy. Alice and I thought we needed more than a media policy . . . " Ilse's voice wobbled a bit. She'd used herself up tonight. She couldn't string her thoughts together any more. She wanted sympathy from Carole, some recognition that she'd fought the good fight. Carole's crack was far from supplying the balm she was looking for. Now she was angry, bone weary, and babbling.

"Ilse, spare me your stream of consciousness and get to the point. Are you coming up or staying home?"

"Everything is stream of consciousness including the Post Office!" Ilse hung up.

The next day Carole called Ilse from her office and apologized. Ilse apologized in return.

Thursday morning at eight-fifteen Dutton was out with his dog, as usual, prancing. As Carole walked behind the pair for a few moments she noticed the dog had a piece of string hanging out of its ass. Getting side by side with the misogynist Carole awarded him her most dazzling smile.

"Mr. Dutton there's a foreign object protruding from your dog's anus."

Dutton's eyes popped then zoomed down to his dog's behind where sure enough a grimy string dangled. Carole left him doubled over his ageing companion trying to lovingly extract the string. Each time he'd give it a pull the dog would yelp and turn a circle. She laughed all the way down to 57th Street where she caught the bus each morning she taught classes. This is going to be a good day, she thought.

Riley, cheery as usual, jerked and jolted her up to the seventh floor. As the door opened she noticed Fred wasn't peering from behind his desk. She reached into her mail box, pulled out all the junk mail and her phone messages. *BonBon called. Important,* read the scrawl. *Adele called. Return call immediately. Ilse called. Urgent.*

"Adele, what's wrong?"

"Have you seen the *Village Rag*?"

"Of course not. I refuse to read that drivel."

"Well, there's a vicious article in it signed by Olive Holloway. Most of the article smears Ilse from one side of Manhattan to another."

"What? Poor Ilse, I'd better call her."

"Wait, Carole. That's not all. This Olive creature doesn't name you by surname but she implies that Ilse is being kept by—and I quote—'A well-heeled art historian by the name of Carole who teaches in one of the city's more prestigious universities.' How many women art historians are there at Columbia, C.C.N.Y., and N.Y.U. who are named Carole? If I ever find this child I am going to hit her up side the head. Are you all right? Do you want me to cancel class and come down there? If there's going to be a fight over your job I want to be there."

"No, Adele, no. Fowler wouldn't dare. I have tenure and I'd like to see him invoke a morals clause on me. I never gave Ilse anything other than dinner and cab fare. Christ, what kind of nut is this Olive?" Carole was more shaken than she sounded.

122

"A pure case of sour grapes, it sounds like. The people who ought to be punished are the *Rag* people for printing anything so irresponsible."

"Listen, Adele. Let me come on over tonight or maybe Ilse and I will both come over if you think it's all right with LaVerne. I want to call Ilse right now. She must be frantic."

"Of course. You're family, don't ask permission, honey. And ring me if anything goes wrong, you hear?"

"Thanks, Adele. Dell—I love you."

"I love you too."

Carole put down the receiver, collected herself, and dialed Ilse.

"Sweetheart?"

"Oh, Carole, Carole, I'm so sorry. I hope you don't think this had anything to do with me. I mean I mentioned you once or twice but never to this woman. She picked it up. Oh please, I hope you don't think this is my fault. I mean, I want you to come out but not like this."

"Ilse, it's all right. It'll take more than a snide implication in pulp to get me in serious trouble here. You're the one. Adele told me most of the article is a broadside aimed at you." Carole hoped what she said was true more than she believed it.

"Yeah, yeah, I know. We called the A.C.L.U. to find out if we have legal recourse. I'm going up there this afternoon to talk to the women in the women's rights division. Olive Holloway is going to get smashed."

"Would you like a bit of advice?"

"Now you sound like my mother."

"There's nothing wrong with that. Mothers have a habit of proving right except you don't find that out until you're the age your mother was when she gave you the advice."

"Okay, you're probably more rational now than I am anyway."

"Forget this. Don't even bother to sue."

"Give up without a fight, never."

"Let me finish. The world is full of Olives. You'll frazzle yourself responding to them. And if you do want to get even with her remember revenge is a dish best served cold. So wait. Maybe by waiting you'll come to understand she isn't worth a reaction from you. Besides the ultimate revenge is your own success. Ignore her and set about your own business. That goes for your entire group."

"Not the group. The least we can do is write a short, noninflammatory letter to the editor. And maybe get a few journalists on our side to call them."

"Perhaps. That's something for you and your group to decide but do listen to me about yourself."

"Yes, ma'm."

"Adele is concerned for you too. Want to go over there tonight with me and we can have supper together?"

"I'd love to. You know I dig Adele and LaVerne but the group will have to meet tonight to decide what we should do. If I get out before two in the morning I'll call to see if you're back home and maybe come on up. Okay?"

"Okay."

As she hung up the phone she heard the elevator door slam and Freddie Fowler whistling. He walked down the corridor to her office, stuck his head in, and chirped, "May I come in?"

"Certainly."

As he took a seat opposite her Carole noticed he had the *Village Rag* tucked under his arm.

"Allow me to close the door, Carole." His voice dropped.

"Fred, I thought you were more subtle than that."

Fred's lips twitched. Carole threw him off balance no matter what he said or did. "Carole, I've read the most disturbing article in the *Village Rag* today and I came directly to you. I want you to know you can confide in me with your, ah, problem. After all, we are in the arts and we're accustomed to this."

"To what, Fred?"

He hedged. "Have you read the article?" God forbid *the word* should escape his lips.

"Let's just say it's been called to my attention."

"I want you to know that, even if this malicious accusation is true, you and I can work things out. We value you here."

"Value me? My reputation enhances a lackluster department. Lay it on the line, Chief."

"Please, there's no call to get hostile. I recognize you must be under a strain."

"Why? Have I reached the age where roommates begin to look suspicious?"

"Now, Carole, I have suspected for some time now that you, that you, perhaps had a different lifestyle than most people."

"Really, I have no idea how most people live. Too broad a subject for me."

"Come on, we've known each other for years. You

can tell me your secret. I've told you it won't affect my regard for you—whether you're keeping this girl or not."

"Possession of a secret is no guarantee of its truth," Carole snapped.

"Well, I didn't mean to suggest that I doubt your word."

"Fred, I am not keeping any 'girl' as you call her. Try woman next time."

Confused, Fred blushed. He wasn't exactly sure why that word was offensive but then he considered himself above such semantic trivia. "I'm terribly sorry. I should have known better."

"What fascinates me is that you won't use the word."

"What word?"

"Lesbian."

Fred's whole body twitched this time. "Uh, it's such an indelicate word. And as you pointed out I have no real reason to even think such a thing. Carole, I'm terribly sorry."

"You should be. For thinking I'm keeping some woman without any evidence other than a slanderous article in a disreputable weekly."

"I hope this little misunderstanding won't affect your regard for me. We've always had such a good working relationship."

"What makes you think I have any regard for you, you pompous ass? You twitter about the department, despotically improving our lot. You sit in your office like a fly rubbing its front feet together every time that elevator door opens and a woman walks out. You've tried to hit on me so many times if I had a

126

nickel for each one I'd be rich by now. And further-more, Fred Fowler, you're so aggressively banal that any time spent with you is dreary—totally dreary."

Immobilized by the torrent, Fred perched in his seat afraid to move even his eyeballs.

"Cat got your tongue, Freddie?"

"You, you're a man-hater. I knew it. I always knew it. No warmth from you. Bitch Dyke." He foamed at the mouth.

"Darling, I haven't the energy to hate men. I'm neutral. You're a minor irritation. Don't let your fool-ish ego blow you up to anything more than what you are, a variety of winged irritant, a fly."

"Castrator."

"You have to be willing to get close to men in or-der to castrate them. I can't be bothered."

"I could have you fired. Homosexuality has yet to be condoned by this university."

"Prove it, Fred. Prove I'm a homosexual."

At this he faltered. "You are."

"Yes, I am. I love women. I have always loved women and I always will and it has next to nothing to do with weaklings like you."

"You said it. You said it. Now I've got you."

"Try it. You lose me and you lose the only pro-fessor of international rank you've got. And what's more, Fred, what does the name Sheila Dzuby mean to you? Or Nan Schonenfeld? Priss Berenson? Oh, the list could go on for ages. You have an unerring instinct for young women whose grade averages need a transfusion, you fastidious vulture. You're in no-man's land. Nan came to me in tears last semester over you. Sheila wanted to report you to the president. You push your luck and see what happens when the sweet young things you've seduced step forward and blow the whistle."

Ashen-faced, Fred rose. His hands trembled and a thin bead of sweat shone on his upper lip. "Why don't we forget this whole unfortunate incident?"

"Fine with me. But one small thing: if I ever hear of you pressuring a student again I'll kick you so hard you'll wear your balls for earrings."

He gulped and slipped out the door. The confrontation shook her too but she didn't know it until Fred left the room.

Even though that slimy creep has been put in his place doesn't mean this thing is over. Who knows how many other people in the department read it? Well, I don't have to worry about Roger; he and Bob Kenin are gay. That leaves four. I might as well be brave about this and get the whole damn thing over with. She went to the tiny office kitchen, took a coke out of the refrigerator, then walked back and knocked on Marcia Gahagan's door. Besides Roger and Bob, Marcia was the only other professor in the department she cared about.

"Come on in."

"Marcia . . . "

"Sit down, Carole. I heard the whole thing. You forget our offices are next to each other. I'm glad you finally nailed the bastard."

Tears came into Carole's eyes. She didn't want to cry but Marcia's hearty response was so needed and so unexpected. Marcia got out of her seat and gave Carole a kleenex.

"Thanks. Lord, I surprise myself. If anyone had

told me I'd react the way I did to Fred then come in here and cry I'd have told her she was crazy. I don't know. Something snapped."

"Carole. For the record, I've known you were a lesbian for a long time and that's your business. There were times when we'd give parties and when I'd ask you I wanted to say, 'Bring your friend,' but I didn't and I'm sorry I didn't. It's silly to be awkward about these things when we're adults. Please forgive me for not being a friend to you a long time ago."

"Thank you." Carole, stunned, reached out to shake her hand and Marcia took it and gave her a good hug.

"Fred won't dare move. I think you're safe."

Carole laughed while wiping her eyes. "I know. I can't bear the gossip that damn article will stir up so I thought I'd go to the other members of the department who don't know and just lay the whole thing to rest."

"Prof. Stowa is so old he'll think you're talking about translating Sappho so you can cross him off. I doubt if the others read that paper and if they do they'll give out some hint and then you can say whatever it is you have to say."

"Sage counsel. Is that clock on your desk on time?"

"Should be."

"I'm five minutes late for class. Thank you again, Marcia."

Carole ran out to the elevator and noticed that Fred had his door closed. The first fruits of victory, she thought.

"That's amazing," LaVerne gasped when Carole finished her story.

"I can't get over Marcia," Adele chimed in. "Familiarity breeds consent."

"Are we keeping score tonight?" LaVerne questioned.

"Love is taking the good with the bad." Carole lifted her palms to heaven.

"And that was a good one. Come on, you two, give me a little credit."

"The funny thing is I feel as though a weight is lifted off my back. I have to give Ilse credit. She was right about coming out."

"Ideally, that should be an individual decision. You had a little help," LaVerne stated.

"You would have had all kinds of help if you'd wanted it. BonBon planned to march down there dressed to hold up traffic as well as a bank and accuse Fred of white slaving," Adele chuckled.

Lester, on the word white, screamed, "Bwana, White Devil."

"Telling me. It took me twenty minutes on the phone to calm her today. She turned out to be more upset than I was."

"It's too bad Ilse couldn't be here. We could all celebrate your day together," LaVerne mentioned.

"We can celebrate on the twenty-ninth when we pick her up from work."

"Adele, you could give me one little hint."

"Go on, give her a teaser."

"Okay. September twenty-ninth is Cervantes' birthday. He was born in 1547. That's a big hint. I'm not telling you another thing."

130

Huddled on the stoop sat Ilse, knees tucked under her chin.

"What are you doing out here?"

"Waiting for you. Anyway, it's such a beautiful night I thought I'd sit out and try to remember what the stars look like."

"How did the meeting go?"

"Terrific. We decided what had to be done and that was that. Then we got into bigger issues."

"Well, what did you decide?"

"That's our secret."

Opening the door to her apartment freed Louisa May who padded down the steps and then bounded back up again.

"Will you sue?"

"Our lawyer talked to them today and they're a little uptight. I'm pretty sure they'll agree to either an apology or an article. But after that business we got into such exciting stuff. Now that Olive's gone people are really talking to each other. We started out trying to define the group and then narrowed it down to the fact that maybe we'd better define ourselves first, you know?"

"Not exactly."

"Well, women have always been without an identity, without a self. We've only been functions, service functions, like a mother or a wife or a secretary. That kind of shit. So if the movement is going to get anywhere fast we have to help women become who it is that they are. See?"

"I always knew who I was. I think you're confusing heterosexual women with women who know they have to earn their own living and who aren't going to get status off of being Mrs. So and So."

"Huh?"

"You can't lump everyone together like that."

"Well, but you have to admit the search for identity is a very real and painful search."

"Bullshit. It's all made up."

Ilse got riled. "What do you mean bullshit? People have to find out who they are. Why do you think there's so much misery in this country?"

"There's misery in this country because most Americans haven't bowed to the nonescapability of causality."

"What?" Ilse squeaked in disbelief.

"People are like children. They don't understand their actions have reactions."

"That's got nothing to do with identity!"

"Oh, yes, it does."

"I'm missing a connection somewhere. I don't see that at all."

"Let me think a minute to see if I can explain it better."

Ilse got up and went to the kitchen. "You want anything?"

"A coke with ice. You know once in a giddy mood I thought ice was the past tense of water. I love that thought."

Ilse didn't see the humor in it if there was any. "Uh huh."

"Let me try it this way, back to identity. Americans believe you can start all over again. That's the whole idea behind upward mobility or downward mobility which is more to the point for your generation.

People want to believe they can wipe their past off the books. Experience isn't shared, it's cut off at the roots. It's lunacy to think your past doesn't bear on your present. In a way that's not accepting the consequences of your actions even if those actions, like where and what you were born, weren't under your control. Does that make sense?"

"It makes sense but you see I think women have to forget the past. We have to be reborn and reject all the old values that kept us subservient."

"So you're advocating an ahistorical movement which means you're doomed to repeat the mistakes of the past. Ilse, be reasonable. You can ask people to transform themselves but you can't ask them to reject what they were without adding to their self-hatred."

"No. Women have to make themselves new."

"Well, honey, I just don't see it that way."

"How can you, you're still stuck back in the Middle Ages? What the hell does the Middle Ages have to do with today?"

"A lot, my dear, a lot. Especially for women."

"This I got to hear."

"The whole idea of courtly love gave women a kind of spiritual power they hadn't known. Men believed the irresistable power of gentleness and beauty, woman, could tame even the most savage beasts. That's why the last of the Unicorn tapestries is so lush. The unicorn was thought to be a ferocious beast—I think it was a symbol for male brutality even if they didn't know it—and here is the unicorn in the lady's lap. She tamed him. And then there's the little problem of the Crusades. Men were away for years, if indeed they ever came back, so women often became lords of the castles and they performed many formerly masculine duties. The merchant class was beginning to stir. The women worked as hard as the men building the business up. In those days who could afford to stay home? The Church remained violently anti-woman and still is, but secular life was changing. It may not seem significant to you, but you're the direct result of it, far away as it may seem."

"So, it's interesting. It's not compelling. I want to get back to this reborn thing. Why should I reclaim my past? Why should I identify with my mother or my father? I reject everything about them. I'm a new person."

"Are you? Isn't your rigidness in denying them the identical rigidness they show to you and your ideas? You're the other side of the same coin and you'd better come to terms with it or you're going to destroy the very thing you care the most about, your movement."

Now Ilse was worried. She feared some dark dragon was about to lumber out from the cave of her subconscious. "You have to be more specific."

"Ilse, you can't be what you aren't. You're not a poor woman. You weren't raised in poverty. You can't go around pretending. I'm not saying you should run back to your mother and play a quick set at Longwood Cricket Club, I'm saying you are more useful to your movement by embracing your background than by rejecting it. Believe me. I spent close to a decade trying to pretend I was an aristocrat. If you say to other women, 'Look, this is what I came from and look how I changed,' then women from that same background will listen to you. And other women might listen too because you're being honest instead of playing poor. If you are reborn what good does it do any of us if we don't know what you were before? You see, you're denying the very power of your movement. You're cutting off your roots and leaving out the eucharist."

"Carole, I'm not too good at religious terms."

"You aren't transmitting to people what it is that changed you. You're not sharing, not giving communion, not communicating that process. Without the process you look very one-sided and very easy to disbelieve."

"I have to think about all this. I can't trust you . . . I mean, I'm always afraid you're trying to belittle my work because you're not in the movement slugging it out and trying to organize. It's hard for me to trust you."

"Ah, so you can't trust anyone who isn't exactly like you are?"

"I . . . Carole, you get me backed into corners. I don't know, maybe that's true. Maybe that's what I'm doing even though I say the opposite. But it's hard to trust women who aren't actively involved in the movement."

"I'm getting involved but in my own way."

"Yeah, but that's what we keep coming back to. People can't go off in their orgies of individualism saying, I'm making the revolution in my own way. For christ's sake, Carole, that leaves the pigs in control of everything."

"I grant you that, but right now there isn't an organization or a project that speaks to me. Maybe it's my age, maybe it's the fact that I've been earning my own way for over twenty-five years now. If something touches me I'll move. Look, I came out today at work because of that damn article."

"You did?"

"Yes, I laid Fred Fowler out to whaleshit."

"I never heard that before."

Carole laughed. "Let's say I'm being true to my roots. I put him over a barrel."

"Will you lose your job?"

"No, I'm one of the lucky ones on that count."

"Carole, I'm really impressed."

"Me, too. People do hear what you say, Ilse, but it takes time and you can't rob me of my individuality by saying, 'Do it this way or you're not one of us!' "

"Carole, I can't buy that. I mistrust the individual thing so much. That's how we've been kept from each other. Every oppressed group is told to bargain with the Man for it's little tidbits. We're told we're individuals, we make it on our own. We have to band together or we're weak."

"I know that much but you can't band people together by telling them to act alike. You know that. It's the idea that has to be shared and certain agreement on projects or whatever. Then people will act on that according to who they are."

"Dammit, that's my point. Women don't know who they are. We are the only oppressed group that has to give people an identity. We didn't live in ghettos, we were kept in the oppressor's house. We have to build those bonds between each other. Our community was destroyed ten thousand years ago."

"And I insist you keep fuzzing the line between

straight women and lesbians."

"There are a lot of lesbians in the movement who don't know who the hell they are either."

"And they're young. Let them go out and earn their living, they'll find out a lot very fast."

"It's not that simple. We have to build an identity on women's values not on men's."

"Jesus christ, Ilse, you can't base salvation on a gene pool. Look at the trouble it brought the Jews."

"Women are different from men and now we have to put each other first."

"I agree. But don't fall into a congenital trap and say we're born different which really means better, right?"

"Right."

"If you exclude men and give them no hope because there isn't anything they can do about it, they'll kill you—out of fear as much as out of hatred."

"That I believe."

"You have to appeal to the mind, to the heart. Don't judge people by their bodies. You have to ask men to become woman-identified, to find and reclaim women's values. I told you, there was a murmur in that direction in the Middle Ages. You can't declare men irrelevant. And I'm not saying most of them aren't complete assholes but you have to give them a chance. That's a damn sight more than they ever gave us."

"Well, I'm not working with them."

"Don't blame you. But twenty years from now or thirty years from now enough of them may be women-identified so there can be solidarity, as you say."

"You've got a sharp mind, Carole. It's too bad you're not actively in the movement."

"Ilse, I've told you a hundred times I hate politics. I'll do what I can do in my field. Or maybe someday I can vote for you."

"Great, that's all I need: my revolutionary fervor dissipated in an electoral illusion."

"I don't understand the mechanics of all that, the difference between revolution and election. Maybe they aren't as far apart as you think. Anyway, what I'm trying to say is someday if we women are called upon to act in unison, I'll do it but I'm not going to organize it or write papers or whatever."

"I am."

"Good. I respect you for it."

"And I can't see a way around giving women new selves."

"Maybe we're purposefully missing each other."

"I'm mad because you discount identity like some grand madam. Maybe it isn't a problem for you because you're forty-four, but it sure is for most of the women I know."

"Ilse, not you, not anybody can set out in search of themself. You can't construct some psychological cathedral. If you do that, well, you ruin whatever it is that's you. If you take cognizance of your identity then you detach yourself from you. You become a spectator to your own life. That's insane. You trap yourself in words. If you sit around thinking about yourself, what you're doing is talking to yourself in English. The language itself will alter you. I don't understand it. I don't understand how this happened so fast. When I was a kid no one ever worried about who they were. You worried about what you were going to do—doctor, lawyer, Indian Chief, that kind of thing—but my god, we never called ourselves into question. And we didn't listen that much to what people said. We watched what they did. Life was immediate. We didn't have to filter everything through the interior mind at work. I can't understand what's wrong with people today. How can anyone possibly think they are going to solve their identity? I swear, self consciousness is original sin."

"Like I said, I have to think about all this."

"Me, too. I feel like we wandered all over the map. Ilse, I don't want to fight with you. I care about you. I'd just like to enjoy the time we have together. Let go. You don't have to carry the entire women's movement every minute of every day."

"I don't know. I feel responsible. I feel I can make a difference and get us on the right track. I feel like I don't even want to sleep. I want to go at it every second."

"You have to relax or you'll be like a vein reducing itself to capillaries. You'll vanish. Besides, people need outside stimulus, relaxation; that's what enriches our work."

"I don't know."

"You won't know until you stop working out of guilt."

"Guilt! What have I got to feel guilty about?"

"Look, I'm sorry I said it. Can't we fall into bed and make love any more without ranging off into some deep discussion?"

"I'm not going anywhere until you tell me about this guilt thing."

"Okay. I think you do believe in this cause. And a big part of you is working for good reasons but a small nagging part of you is guilty, that's why you don't relax. Stop trying to even the score. You were born with money. That's not your fault. Make use of it, don't deny it. Anyone who puts you down for your birth is full of shit—whether they're poor or rich themselves. It's what you do with your life that's important, not what you couldn't help—your sex or your color or money. You deserve respect for what you're doing, not condemnation because you were born with a lot of advantages. Look at all the rich people who do nothing with their lives. So be proud of yourself."

"I think I have a lot to learn, Carole. And I'm sorry I seem to learn by fighting with you. I don't know why I do that and I want to stop but I know I'll do it again."

"I did it too. I used to fight with my parents all the time and pick on my friends at school. We all do it. It's easier to call the other person an idiot than to look at our own blunders. Don't be so serious, honey; come on. Let's go to bed."

Carole put her hands on Ilse's face and kissed her. The young woman threw her arms around her neck and held her for what seemed like ten minutes. Then they took a shower and quietly went to bed making love like dreamers in a river, borne by the current rather than simple desire.

LaVerne stood in front of the bird cage coaxing Lester with bits of dried apricot.

"Lester, come on now. Piss, shit. Say it."

Unfurling his headdress he waddled back and forth on his branch clucking and turning his head nearly upside down to see if the other birds were noticing. The mynah, wildly interested in the fruit, said, "It's the real thing," and that set Lester off for fear he'd be overshadowed. LaVerne gave the mynah a piece of fruit and Lester practically molted on the spot.

"Come on, Lester, snap to it. Do it for Aunt LaVerne. Piss, shit . . . "

Lester puffed out his white breast, "Piss, shit, corruption, snot. Twenty-four dupers tied in a knot. Apeshit, batshit, fuckaroo. All you girls lay down and screw!"

"LaVerne, are you in there with that bird again?"

"We're having a meaningful conversation."

"Since when is 'apeshit, batshit' meaningful?"

Just then, Lester uttered quite distinctly, "Each against all."

Adele exasperated, "What the hell is that?"

"That's the Twelfth Commandment, sweetheart."

Throwing her hands to heaven, Adele pleaded, "Why me, God, why me?"

LaVerne answered in a deep voice, "Because you piss me off."

"That joke is so old it's got gray hairs. You spend more energy teaching that damn Lester dirty things to say. We'll never be able to give a party. Plus the mynah's picking it up."

"These birds learn faster than half the kids did in my third grade class," LaVerne noted.

"Just goes to prove that we humans are highly overrated."

"Do you need any help?"

"No, I've got most of it under control. The damn car rental place won't let us use BonBon as a chauffeur. I can't decide whether to rent someone's private Rolls or whether to do without Bon as the driver."

"Will she be upset if she doesn't drive?" LaVerne asked.

"I don't think so. As long as she's in on some of the fun she doesn't care in what capacity."

"That's good. Decided what you're going to wear?"

"That clingy thing you gave me. I think it's the soul of the 1930's. What about you?"

"Give me five minutes and I'll show you. Don't follow me in the room. Let me surprise you and if you don't like it then I can change to something else."

LaVerne raced into the bedroom and closed the door. Lester was crawling up the side of the cage then swinging by his bill. Apricots brought out his athletic nature. Lester adored Adele and she fussed over him while waiting for LaVerne. He liked to stick his tongue out at her and she'd pretend to grab it. Then he'd say, "Pretty boy," and nod his head up and down. LaVerne opened the bedroom door and appeared in a pale yellow chiffon dress with a broad brimmed hat. She walked right out of the twenties.

"Honey, where'd you come out?"

"The Cotton Bowl."

"Gorgeous. Stunning. That is so gorgeous. Really, you look like a debutante on her way to the final bash. And that yellow makes your skin glow. Damn, now I don't know what to wear."

"Adele, I thought you were going to wear the blouse I gave you?"

"Well, I was but I'm outclassed. I have to think of

something better."

"Let's go through the closet and use our imaginations."

After an hour and a half of combinations Adele decided upon a blood red jumpsuit with wide legs and a wide black sash. She also decided to use the regular Rolls rental.

A shining highhat Rolls picked up Adele and LaVerne promptly at seven p.m. On the way over to Carole's they fiddled with all the gadgets in the back then stared regally out the windows and enjoyed watching people crane their necks to see who could be in the car. As the car glided to a halt in front of Carole's, Adele told the driver to honk the horn. What could be more perfect, she thought, than to have your date beep for you? She was sorry she hadn't remembered to buy furry dice to hang on the rear view mirror. The door opened and Carole froze on the steps. Adele rolled down the window and yelled, "Get your ass in here, Mary, we've got a full itinerary."

Carole dazzled in a floor length gown. Simply cut, it had a plain round neck, tight long sleeves, and a line that followed her body. The deep midnight blue was electrified by a half magenta sunburst that started at the collar on her right side and one ray ran in an ever thinning line down her right sleeve, the other rays beamed through the dark blue body. She carried no purse and when she bent her tall figure over to get into the car, Adele said, "See, LaVerne, I told you. Royalty never carries money."

"I have it in my shoe along with my Virginia state driver's license which I've faithfully renewed since I was sixteen."

"Carole, that is the most beautiful thing I've ever seen. It's perfect for you. Where did you ever buy it?" LaVerne stroked the fabric.

"One day I was looking through old costume books . . . I think the fashions in the twelfth and thirteenth centuries were so magnificent and I got the idea to design this dress. Since you and Adele have been after me to bedeck myself, I took it to a designer friend of mine at Vera's and she did it. Her work is exquisite."

"Driver, to MacDonald's on 70th and Second Avenue," Adele directed.

"Adele?" LaVerne couldn't believe her ears.

"We're going to load up on shit food and eat it on our way to the theater. I'll bet you never ate a Big Mac in the back seat of a Rolls."

The driver double parked between 70th and 69th right in front of MacDonald's and Adele, after taking everyone's order, rushed in. People came out of the place to look at the car. Just as many stayed in to look at Adele. She came out and crawled in the car, calling out orders like a curb waitress. "Wait a minute. Just wait before you expose one of those burgers. LaVerne, reach back and give me the towels. There now, cover yourselves in the towels because I don't want you to slop food all over yourselves. Okay, on to the theater."

As they pulled up in front of an off-Broadway theater that must have been an old burlesque house, Adele warned the driver under no circumstances to throw away their MacDonald's litter.

"Man of La Mancha," a big hit in the middle sixties,

144

was being revived. Even the theater's immediate past seemed a better risk than the present. Most producers had lost their courage. Regardless of the reason the play was preferable to the latest 1916 revival lighting up Broadway. As it was Cervantes' birthday, Adele considered the play's reappearance a stroke of good luck.

After the play, Adele ordered the driver to head for the Plaza.

"What are you up to now? The play was enough," Carole exclaimed.

The great hotel loomed into view, an expensive relic, holding court at the southeast end of Central Park. As the gleaming car pulled around the white fountain, the doorman anticipated their stop, expecting perhaps baggage or at least the emergence of the occupants who would then disappear into one of the overpriced eateries. A Rolls has a magnetic quality: once again people waited on either side of the red carpet to see what celebrity would come forth and reveal some fatal flaw, a sagging bustline perhaps or an obvious toupee.

With the air of one who regularly deals with the rich, the doorman in his phony Prussian uniform opened the door.

Adele stuck her face out and said, "Hi, you all. We just dropped by," and dumped all the MacDonald's Big Mac wrappers, french-fry holders, milkshake containers, and dirtied napkins right there at his feet. The fellow let go of the door in horror—this was as ghastly as the assassination at Sarajevo—and Adele unceremoniously stretched out a blood red arm and closed the door. The driver floored it and they barrelled down Fifth Avenue, the three women roaring from the spectacle.

"Adele, whatever possessed you to do this?"

She looked at Carole and LaVerne and said, wiping moisture from her eyes, "I came to the conclusion that most people give up their dreams by calling them fantasies. All that's left of their lives is a dusty survival in old telephone directories. Once in a great while we have to let fly or we atrophy. So I'm making one evening the way I want it."

"You know, you're right, honey. If people have surrendered their dreams then they're keeping up with the Jonses who can't keep up with themselves."

"Ah, so tonight is a night of destiny," Carole laughed.

"Let's hope we don't meet our destiny on the road. Driver slow down up there," Adele commanded.

"Where are we going now?" LaVerne questioned her.

"Wait and see. The unexpected keeps the human race from stagnation."

"There she is laying down those heavy lines of life." LaVerne squeezed Adele's elbow.

Rumbling down the pitted streets of the Manhattan bridge, the car seemed to the riders to be able to keep them safe from the desolation of the lower East side. They crossed over the bridge and the driver took a side street into Brooklyn Heights, depositing them as close to the Promenade as possible. From there they could view all of Manhattan, a dark honeycomb dotted with lights.

"The buildings look like a Titan's dominos," Carole remarked.

146

"I can never gaze at this city without a sense of awe. It's the best and the worst," followed LaVerne.

"I always think of it as the altar of corporate vision . . . the city that money built. I wonder, if an ancient Mayan could see it, what would she think?"

"Especially if she had to go to the bathroom. Ever notice how Americans build cities with absolutely no regard for how our bodies function?" LaVerne said.

"That's because we live amid the remains of architectural imagination, Vern. This is the city of post-human reference."

"That may be so but I think LaVerne is trying to tell us she has to relieve herself," Adele noted.

"You mean the Rolls doesn't have a built-in bathroom?"

"This is as good a time as any to head for our next stop where such matters can be attended to."

The next stop was a gay bar on Sheridan Square, the Queen's Drawers. As usual people stopped to see who would be getting out of the car. Adele led the procession like a secular cardinal. She didn't especially like the bar but where else could they go? She hadn't the money to rent Roseland. As it was she had to bribe the manager to put a few unusual records on the juke box. "The Blue Danube" was not often heard at places like this. BonBon and Creampuff held down a table near the dance floor. They applauded when the threesome approached like gradations of the rainbow.

"Where's the Pope?" BonBon bellowed on seeing Adele.

"Punching holes in prophylactics so there'll be

more Catholics," Adele answered.

They seated themselves, ordered drinks, and caught up on who did what, when, and to whom.

"Where's Maryann?" LaVerne asked Bon.

"When last seen she was heading west on a tricycle with a flat."

"Yeah," Creampuff added, "she went to Chicago for an audition but she'll return next weekend. She sends her love on Quixote's birthday. Isn't that what you're celebrating?"

"Sort of," Carole agreed.

"Jesus, listen to that music: Palm Beach mortuary style. After this dance they'll have to take a body count," BonBon grumbled.

" 'Ritual Fire Dance' isn't on the box. Think you'll manage?" Adele teased.

"Better than 'Camptown Races.' "

Creampuff stopped the conversation with, "Did you hear Pat Smith's friend died today? She choked to death on a chicken bone."

"Ha," BonBon interjected, "that old dyke swallowed a fur ball."

LaVerne, shocked, admonished her, "How can you say such a thing?"

"Because it's true. That old broad did so much muff diving we should have bought her scuba equipment. Anyway, I hated her."

"Whatever for?" Carole asked. "She run out of oxygen on you?"

"No, she sold us a fake early American painting and she did it on purpose. If she'd have asked for the money we'd have given it to her but she made a fool out of us, dammit."

148

"Are we going to see the Rolls Royce?" Creampuff changed her own subject.

"Sure, when we leave," Adele told her.

"Next thing I know, Dell, you'll buy an estate on the Hudson River, you're getting such expensive tastes—like the landed gentry," Bon sniffed.

"I'm starting my own back-to-the-land movement," Adele replied, "and buying cemetery plots."

Carole laughed. "That's right. My mother always told me, 'Buy land; if there's a war you can fill in the potholes.' "

BonBon, slightly out of joint, went back to the faults of the departed. "She used to masturbate on chairs. God knows how she did it. Maybe I'm dumb or missing something. Anyway, the first time I was ever in her house I had to ruthlessly stifle an urge to wiggle on all the chairs to see if it works. Besides that she wore prison matron shoes. I could never look down at her feet without thinking of the time Creampuff and I landed in the pokey for lewd conduct."

Adele whispered to Carole, "I don't know why but picking up pieces of Bon's diatribe reminds me of the men who were arrested for exposing themselves in the snake cage at the Bronx zoo. Remember when the papers carried that story?"

"Was your Big Mac laced with opium?"

Creampuff spiced Bon's tale about the jail: " . . . even when she was parked she was a moving violation, that's what the pigs said, the fuckers."

"Let's dance." Carole motioned for everyone to get up and shut up.

However, dancing produced a high-octane reaction in BonBon. She became Motor Mouth. "Did I ever

149

tell you how we got out of the business?" And before waiting for a reply she launched away, "Creampuff and I were working at the King of Clubs down in D.C. Oh, D.C. was a hot strip-town back then—all covered by the cops, of course. All those government types used to come and jerk off as soon as they'd hear the first drum roll. Creampuff's specialty was the slow peel." Creampuff demonstrated to the applause of the onlookers. BonBon continued, "Drove the rednecks bananas. My big number was a take-off of Sally Rand and her fans. Top billing, and the costume . . ."

Creampuff interrupted. "You shoulda' seen her. She wore a long black wig put up in a French twist. Elegance. Her costume, such as it was, was emerald green to accent her eyes and her spike heels made her as tall as Carole Hanratty."

BonBon regained the floor by upping her volume. "That's important now. Remember spike heels back in 1956? For a year or two there was a fad of steel high heels figuring they wouldn't wear out as fast as that cardboard crap they passed off as shoes. Used to do my routine to the 'Ritual Fire Dance.' Drove them wild. Absolutely wild. Well, the King of Clubs had light sockets on the stage floor. Lots of old stages do, ya know. So it was twelve midnight. Creampuff slithered off the boards and I was shivering in the wings waiting for my cue. The music starts, you've all heard that beginning."

In case they hadn't, Creampuff hummed the tune and supplied the drum rolls. Adele fought valiantly to choke back an explosive laugh as her voice wiggled up and down on the high notes and Creampuff couldn't resist a little hip action when she made a boom sound.

150

Carole couldn't look at Adele or they would have squealed like grade school kids looking at a picture of genitals.

"Beautiful, honey," BonBon said in a firm voice.

Creampuff kept on adding more and more English to her drum rolls.

Her voice somewhat sharper, "Beautiful, honey. They all remember the song now. The footlights came up and the spot picked me up as my leg kicked out in front of the curtain. The boys dug that. Really dug it. Legs were important then. Now it's all tits and teeth. Was I hot that night. Could do no wrong. Yes, I was the Jane Russell of strip. Well, honeys, right in the middle of my number I stepped in a light socket and the juice hits me so hard my wig flies off into the audience and I can't move! Ya know electricity holds you. I hung there on that socket, my heel stuck in it, vibrating like I had St. Vitus's dance. The boys went wild. Those asswipes thought it was part of the show. They're whistling and throwing money and shouting 'Hot Mama' and who knows what else. I was so scared I didn't know whether to shit, run, or go blind. I'd a died out there if Creampuff hadn't run over to the board and thrown all the switches."

"I saw my baby out there being electrocuted and I want to tell you I took off like a shot. Knocked down the stage manager, a greasy old fart who weighed three-fifty if he weighed a pound, charged to the switches right behind the curtain there, and hit everything at once. The house went dark and the guys musta' been creaming in their supporters because they thought by now she was in the altogether. I ran out there on the stage and threw my silk sequined cape

151

over BonBon who couldn't speak, my god, she was half-fried. We'd been together for about four years then and I thought I was losing the only person in the world who made life worth living. I was bawling and sobbing and stroking her forehead, telling her I loved her and she'd pull through. I promised Jesus my G-string and Virgin Mary my pasties. Management kept the lights down, of course. Imagine if those sock jocks found out most of us chippies were queer? I don't know when the ambulance came but I hit the attendant over the head when he tried to keep me out of the back and I crawled in, in full drag mind you, sparkles all through my hair to say nothing of the feathers, and I held Bon's hand the whole way. I didn't care who knew." Creampuff finished out of breath with the violence of her recalled emotion. "That was that," Bon picked up the thread. "I figured the Good Lord was trying to tell me something so I quit the business and opened my antique shop up on 62nd and Second. Business has been good to us and we have a lovely apartment and the house in the Pines."

What BonBon didn't tell was that even in the hospital after the shock she kept her nails long, teased her hair, and put on a full face by noon promptly. She began to see shadows in her mirror when putting on her Revlon nonsmear mascara. BonBon became convinced there were spirits in the room. Not hostile ghosts but spirits trying to tell her something about what to do with her life. Since that time she developed into a closet mystic. Only Creampuff knew how deeply she felt about astrology and the occult. Her friends had the faintest whiff of it when she asked their signs, rising and so forth. Carole told her she was a Sagittarius with temperatures rising but Bon-Bon wheedled her birth date and place out of her and discovered Carole to be a Sagittarius with Libra rising. Adele was an Aries with Libra rising. Bon kept their charts yearly and silently nodded to herself whenever they confirmed her computation by some significant action like the purchase of a painting or catching the flu. But her own life remained a mystery to her and Bon could never quite be sure why she was put on earth. She decided her mission was to bring joy to her friends and quietly watch over their fortunes like an ancient Aztec scanning the stars.

Bon chattered on, punctuated by Creampuff's laughter. They never tired of one another. The other inhabitants of the bar, while not exactly spring chickens, were a good deal younger than the dancing group. They stared at the dancers. Their manners and their elegant clothes gave the impression that the older women were slumming. Such women rarely visited the Queen's Drawer where New Jersey meets the Bronx and lives happily ever after, where the toilets overflowed each night at midnight, and where Marijane Kerr, an old barfly known to all lesbians, had personally painted the plunger with the word *Ladies* in jungle-red nail polish.

How incongruous that they should be in here and after such a night. But then Adele believed in the sovereignty of the incongruous. Checking her watch hidden under her sleeve, she whispered to Carole that it was time to pick up Ilse from Mother Courage.

As they pulled up in front of the restaurant Ilse was in the doorway shouting at a persistent man. They rolled down the windows and the fragrance of

153

cheap wine hit them in the face. He couldn't walk too well either. There he stood lurching in the doorway while Jill Ward, in a purple undershirt that displayed well-developed arms, quietly moved over to back up Ilse. Two angry faces were too much for him but he managed to garble at full volume as he stumbled off, "Juss what do you women want, anyway?"

"Colorado," Ilse barked. She noticed the car as he staggered away.

Adele called out, "Greetings, salutations, and all other forms of hello. Get in, we'll take you both home."

Jill, laughing, with her hands on her hips, answered, "No thanks. I'm waiting for Dolores to pick me up."

Ilse, amazed, came over to the car and looked at Carole.

"What the hell is this?"

"Adele's surprise. Surprised? We've been off tilting windmills. Come on."

"I can't be seen riding in this thing."

"Then lie on the floor," Adele told her flatly.

Reluctantly Ilse climbed in and hunched on the floor. Not much was said on the way home. Carole embraced Adele and LaVerne as she and Ilse arrived at the well-kept brownstone apartment building.

"Thank you for the unexpected."

"My pleasure." Adele kissed her.

As they drove off LaVerne said, "Looks like a fight."

"Yep."

Adele pulled her favorite wing chair over to the glass doors in front of the garden. She often liked to sit up late reading, writing, or puzzling in the rare silence of the night. LaVerne woke up each day at seven whether she had to go to work or not. They adjusted over-time to each others internal time clock. Adele would wake up somewhere between ten and eleven and, if it was Saturday or Sunday, LaVerne greeted her with a hot cup of tea as she padded out of the bathroom.

Adele thought, it's the little things that keep you together. My mother told me that when I used to ask her how she got along with Daddy. I didn't listen to Mother. Well, I always was a smartass. What was my rallying cry at T.J. High? 'Yeast in the drain traps. Cherry bomb the toilets.' Smartass. Should of listened to Mom—would have saved me the heartbreak of my divorce. Funny word, but papers or no papers, divorce is the same. LaVerne taught me the small kindnesses of everyday life that gradually overwhelm a grandiose act of generosity. The tea in the morning, paying attention to my clothes, fussing over me if I put on a pound. Sometimes I think I don't do as much for Verne as she does for me. I forget sometimes. I do take her out to dinner once a week at least, and movies whenever there's one we like. I massage her feet when she's had a hard day. I wonder how I lived before LaVerne? I can't even remember. Seems like some dim, uncertain fog. She taught me that each day is the only day. I must find beauty in the day, correct a wrong if I can, fulfill my obligations to my friends, my people, even my country. I can never treat a day as cheap or expect there will be another one. LaVerne calls me "the brain" but she's the one who taught me what's most important to know. Carole has that but doesn't transmit it. No, that's not fair. I've never lived with her or perhaps I'd have picked it up. LaVerne's background isn't all that far from Carole's, a little higher up with money. Maybe that knowledge, that gift is something all poor or near-poor people have: the ability to savor the moment, to laugh out loud.

Mom gave me good advice but for a long time I couldn't listen. Their battle for whiteness, for respectability is almost heroic if it weren't so sad. Maybe that's why I couldn't listen. There they are sitting in St. Louis in that goddamned mansion on that private street. Every two years without fail, Dad buys a Cadillac. To this day I can't look at a Cadillac without embarrassment. How vulgar. Couldn't he buy something less gigantic, less Midwestern? And every two years he buys Mother what he calls "a little runabout for my sugar," usually a small-model Buick. Even the runabout can't fall into the low-priced three. There they sit surrounded by color televisions in the upstairs and downstairs, a small black and white one in the bathroom, electric can openers, electric carving knives, electric face moisturizers, hot combs, blenders, automatic ice crushers. If it's new and it's got a button they buy it. And Daddy's expensive golf clubs. Mom's a golf widow. She retaliated by taking up tennis. And what astounds me, what knocks me out is that they're happy. Or maybe they only think they're happy. Don't they know they're supposed to be miserable? I feel waste amid all the appliances. I have yet to meet two more perversely cheerful people. They've made it. They sit among all the things that prove they've won. I don't think they've won but they do. I guess that's what's important. The crowning blow is they're Republicans. The next thing I know they'll throw a sit-down dinner for two hundred: tents and music to honor Sammy Davis, Jr. Well, I guess I'm the snob. They didn't teach me what I wanted to learn but they gave me my chance. I wouldn't be where I am now if they hadn't wanted me to make something out of myself. To go farther than they did. They worship money and I turned to the lost beauties of another time. Verne's right, I don't give them enough credit. I developed my so-called refined sensibility even if in reaction because of them. Who the hell am I to sit in judgment of my parents, anyway? Dad buys a Cadillac and I rent a Rolls. How'd I get on this jag?

Is that what fascinates me about the Mayas? We see exquisite temples but how did they feel about their parents? Did a woman bring her friend a drink in the morning? I never felt how pressing was the presence of the dead until I went up eighty-four hundred feet and saw Machu-Picchu. There wrapped in clouds sat the fortress city guarded by the Andes standing like sentinels. What a sight! Up to that time my work was the usual blend of curiosity stiffened by pedantry. But after that I was humbled before our ancestors. They're all our ancestors. And the Mayas were the Inca's ancestors prefiguring Machu-Picchu. I know it's a cliche but I can't help falling back on it: we're a human chain. The dead give to the living and the living must give to each other and we must secure the future for the unborn. The thought comforts me.

If I get torn apart in my own time or confused, I at least know I have my place in time. I'm part of this chain. We have a few scraps of Mayan thought. I think the most beautiful is, "Life is a conversation between all living things." I amend that for myself to include those who went before me and those who come after. Perhaps I was drawn to study these people to learn this. I'm not sure I could have learned it if I remained bound to my own century. I'm an incredibly lucky woman.

She got up with tears in her eyes and tiptoed to the bedroom so she wouldn't wake up LaVerne.

"A Rolls Royce!"

"Ilse, I had nothing to do with it but if I had I wouldn't be ashamed of it."

"For chrissake, a Rolls is the symbol of class oppression. I can't believe you ignore things like that."

"A symbol doesn't equal oppression. My riding in a Rolls Royce doesn't make me one of the four hundred."

"Just because you're not one of them doesn't mean you don't identify with them. Don't you know that's the secret of American control? The rich get the nonrich to identify with them."

"You're making a mountain out of a molehill."

"No, I'm not. The symbols of the rich have no place in my life. I don't identify with rich people and I don't want other people to identify with them or to lump me with them either. Gucci or Rolls or whatever, it's all the same to me: disgusting. How can I ride around in a car like that or wear Tiffany earrings? I can't believe you can't see it."

"I don't give a damn what other people think."

"Yeah, I know. You're above all that. Above the struggle and beside the point."

"Oh, come on now. This is all out of proportion to the incident. I ride in a fancy car one night and you've got me owning all of South America."

"It's not trivial. Don't act so consciously reasonable. That infuriates me almost as much as you riding around in that damn car. It's patronizing. I'm trying to make you understand that you can't take these things for granted. It's a new time. People who ride in big cars are objects of hate these days in a way they never were before. Well, I don't know about the Depression, I mean how people were emotionally. But from what I can see these things like cars and alligator shoes are no longer neutral things. What you do affects other people in a way you don't seem to understand."

"One night in that ludicrous car is hardly going to affect anyone, except you."

"Well, I'm important. But you're trying to trivialize again. More people than myself saw you in that car."

"Ilse . . ."

"Let me finish. What did Jill Ward think? I can just see this dumb story circulating all through the movement."

"If your getting in the car is so gossip worthy then the movement sounds to me like a disguised *kaffee-klatch*."

Ilse paused and sighed. "Unfortunately, sometimes it leans in that direction. I console myself with the fact that gossip seems to oil the machinery of any political group whether it's on the Hill or us. Not much consolation though. I guess I want people to act like they should instead of how they do."

Carole turned on the stereo and Bobby Short sang "So Near Yet So Far."

"Look, I've told you a thousand times, I don't give a damn what other people think. I want to live my life as I see fit."

"And I keep telling you that you confuse individualism with independence."

"Whenever you get on my case I have the distinct impression you want us all in uniform. Hell, I'm beginning to think individuality went out with the French Revolution."

"Jesus, what are you, campaigning for reactionary of the year?"

"I don't know. I want out of the shadow of the guillotine."

"Very cute. And I'm not suggesting we all wear uniforms although it'd give me a certain thrill to see Seventh Avenue fall to pieces. I'm saying we have to have some communality. And we have to have discipline. That's not the same as saying everyone has to look alike, act alike, think alike. Without community and discipline we'll stay ineffective fragments or worse, we'll be obliterated."

"I'm not a political person. All I want is to be left alone to do my work."

"You damn sight better become a political person. Things are so bad no one can afford to sit on the sidelines."

"Ilse, I've had about enough of this. Now this is my last word on the subject. First of all, there are no

160

organizations which represent my interests. Nobody wants their queers. Not Blacks, whites, rich, poor, women or men. We're outcasts. So you've organized lesbians. Fine and good except they're all under thirty. At least all the ones I've seen are young. If they're not under thirty then they're as downwardly mobile as the postwar generation was upwardly mobile. I'm not going to trade in my Ph. D. for a workshirt and tie-dye jeans. I'm forty-four years old. My interests are different. So you all may be doing something useful. I mean, I know you're doing something useful but it's not anything I can participate in. And even if there were a group close to my interests, I might give money but I don't know if I'd give time. I'm not a joiner. I don't like being subject to human limitation and when you've thrown in your lot with a group that's exactly what happens. You move at the pace of the slowest instead of the fastest. I've got this one fragile life and I have to fight enough things without spending the next three years explaining policy to someone who can't or doesn't want to understand it."

"Our entire society's falling apart. I can't understand that you don't give a shit."

"Society isn't falling apart. It never was together."

"You're impossible!" Ilse stormed out and slammed the door.

Louisa May rushed to the door but she was late. Carole picked the cat up and kissed her forehead. The buzzer rang.

"It's me. I forgot my bag."

Ilse ran up the stairs and Carole handed the gas mask bag to her. She said, "Thank you," and looked as though she wanted to say more, then gave up on it.

Carole quietly closed the door as Ilse walked back down the carpeted stairs. She resisted the impulse to open the street side windows and watch Ilse disappear in the direction of Park Avenue.

Well, it had to happen, she thought to herself. We were two right people who met at the wrong time, that's all. Or maybe we were two right people who were born at the wrong times. It isn't that I disavow her cause. I can't make the same choice she's made. I don't know. She allows for no compromises. Surely, there's such a thing as an honest compromise of thought. Maybe that's her years. The young are notoriously intolerant although it's the old that are blamed for it. She doesn't seem to understand or care that there's a difference between ideology and the truth. Well, her logic is compelling even if it isn't always based on reality. No, that's not fair. I'm not being fair at all. Much of what she says is true. But she jumps off from simple discrimination into an interlocking system of sexism, racism, capitalism, and god knows what else. Maybe it's all connected but right now I find much of her thinking impermissibly vague. Maybe it's me. But I can't take her say-so on faith. If all these things are connected then I need to see those connections. That's not too much to ask. Any thinking person who isn't overly political would ask the same question. Just because a woman says something doesn't mean I'm bound to believe her. I want proof. I'm a rational being. Head before heart. Thank god. If there's one thing I despise it's irrationality. That's really what's wrong between Ilse and me. She says the same thing over and over again thinking repetition will substitute for proof. Dammit, I'm not taking anything on faith. And I know the women's movement is young and Ilse is young but they'd both better do their intellectual homework.

Fortified by what she thought was the compelling purity of her own logic, Carole set about straightening up her desk, ignoring the loneliness creeping up on her. Bobby Short's records were followed by Cris Williamson. The sound of a woman's voice filling the background increased her loneliness although she was unaware of it.

She marched into her bedroom followed by the two fat cats. Turning down the covers she noticed a pale yellow pubic hair on the white sheet, a reminder of lovemaking past. Christ, how can anyone get sentimental over a pubic hair? She picked it up and went into the bathroom where she threw it in the wastebasket. She washed her face and hands. Dried them and looked into her small three-way mirror as she put on her night cream. She paused, momentarily captured by her own image.

How delicious. Am I going to sit here and gaze at my forty-four-year-old face in an orgy of concern over my ageing equipment? Trite, trite and boring, the confrontation of woman with mirror. How many movies have I seen where the once great beauty goes into a fit looking at herself? For some reason a woman contemplating her face is the equivalent of a man frothing at the mouth about the state of the universe and his own soul. I don't even think Katherine Hepburn pulled it off in "The Lion in Winter."

Yet for all her sarcasm she stayed with the smooth reflection. It wasn't vanity holding her there. A fear gripped her. She feared looking into her own eyes

163

but, prompted by hidden voices, she slowly raised her head full upright and raised her eyes into her own stare. Silence. The pupil widened as though a stone had been thrown in the middle of her blackness. The ripples raced to the unseen. The self retreated under such scrutiny. But what retreat was there in a three-way mirror revealing an infinite regress of self? She couldn't see the end of her image. She no longer knew what she believed at this moment. And if she no longer knew, who was that in the mirror?

A bag of bones. Yes, a bag of bones. She congratulated herself on her own humor in the loss of self. Or was she so full of self that there was no self? Had she circled and circled her perimeter until she diminished to zero? The joke was short lived and the reflection grew tears. If she no longer knew what she believed or even if she had a self she could still feel. The reverberation of a heartbeat threatened to break her entire delicate structure. Her eyes left the engulfing pupil and followed a tear as it splintered around the corners of her mouth.

Here I am slipping into self doubt. I rarely allow myself to cry. I always wonder am I indulging myself in some exotic melancholy or is it weakness? I've always detested tears. How I wanted to strangle Mother when she'd break into those huge, titanic sobs that would shake the house. Tears are traitors. They rob me of my strength. If I hold them back I can hold together. And here I am bawling. I can stand the pain. I just can't stand to see it. God, if only I could go back where I came from. Then I could haul off and belt Luke or Margaret, steal one of their bicycles, and ride until I couldn't pedal anymore. The exhaustion

164

purged me of whatever pain or hatred there was. That's all gone now. I lost it somewhere between eighth grade and ninth, between grade school and high school. The world was lusty red and thunderous black. You knew where you stood. You knew how to fight back or lie and then go do it again. Sweet jesus, how far have I wandered from my roots that I could be muffled like this? How much have I pushed back, choked, smoothed over in order to win? And I haven't even won. I shouldn't quibble with Ilse. For all the petty disagreements, the real reason I fought her was because I don't want to look at the span of years between eighth grade and now. I want myself back. I want to knock the shit out of someone I don't like. I want to play kick the can at twilight. I want to laugh without knowing it's going to stop. I'm so tired. I'm so tired of the people around me, except for Adele. I don't want to explain anything to anyone. I don't need a reason. I didn't need a reason when I was a kid. Chocolate ice cream tasted good. Who cared about calories? We knew each other then. If I looked in a mirror it was to wash my face.

She pushed herself away from the mirror over the sink. And then she slowly crumpled underneath it and had a good cry.

The cold, unimaginative richness of Park Avenue in the seventies and sixties fired Ilse as much as the Rolls Royce. She walked faster than usual, scowling.

I learned my lesson. I repeat the same mistake over and over. It doesn't work out with a woman who's not a feminist yet. I keep hoping that it will but the change is too great and the challenge too much for them. The only way they can defend their ego, that piece of them built to survive all the shit, is to disagree with me. This always happens. I keep thinking some woman out there will make the transition without such a hassle. They turn into feminists but first they have to resist you. It's exhausting. I really don't want to ever go through it again. Carole will get it together. I know she will. Off my back. I wonder if that's what happened in other places. You can read all you want but the books never tell how a Chinese peasant changed into a soldier. What happened inside? By this time there are hundreds of thousands of us and we can tell each other what happened but we can't seem to tell people not with us yet. We try or at least I try and all I get is no. I'm not patient. I just lay it on the line. I'm no good at it. I've seen Alice go through this same resistance from people but she's calm. She holds their hand practically while they cling to their outworn beliefs. Well, I haven't got that one-to-one talent. And I'm not very attentive. I only want to bother with people when I feel like it even when I love them. When I watch lovers together I always feel like they're playing hostess to each other. I could never give anyone that suffocating attention. Carole never asked for that. Come to think of it she never asked for much of anything. She has a funny kind of reserve. At first I thought she was some kind of aristocrat. But now I think I like that in her. I could use some of that distance myself. She taught me some valuable things, really. Maybe in time we can be friends or something. There's too much friction to be lovers but who knows? I did learn from her. What is it she used to tell me when I'd start speed rapping?

Oh yeah, "Words are the oil slick on the waters. Integrity holds truth to be more complex than language." She's a brilliant woman. Maybe the Buddists are right. When you're ready your teacher comes. I think I taught her too. She just doesn't know it yet.

God, I hate these fucking buildings. They're inhabited by moral lepers. How can anyone miss the rot here? The few who live off the many. I hate these people. I hate everything they stand for and I hate their Mercedes Benzes and Rolls Royces. I hate their suntanned cadavers and the sickening smile on their faces. And the women who live here. They're worse than the pigs they married. Maybe because I expect more of them. Diamonds. They actually wear diamonds on their fingers and ears and over their breasts. If we had all the diamonds located on Park Avenue between 79th and 60th Streets, we could finance rape crisis centers in every major city in this country and probably still have money left over. We've got to end their hold on this country. What good are civil rights when they run everything? These people are the enemy. Here and on Fifth Avenue and Grosse Pointe and Brookline and Bel Air and Beverly Hills and wherever they congregate with their fat cars loitering in the driveways like shiny cockroaches.

What few women there were on the streets when Ilse emerged from the subway at Sheridan Square blurred into replicas of Carole. All voices became her voice. She thought maybe Carole hurried down here to apologize. She crossed Grove Street and opened the first door leading into the Queen's Drawers and nearly got squashed as a party of five barreled out of the second inner door. When she walked inside the place all heads at the bar turned, then resumed conversation. The coat attendant, eager for the small sum each checked coat brought the house, grabbed at Ilse's light jacket.

"No, I don't want to check my coat. I'm looking for someone."

"That's what they all say but okay, honey."

The dance floor was occupied but not crammed. After ten minutes of searching Ilse walked back out into Sheridan Square.

It was a dumb idea. If she's looking for me she wouldn't go into the bar, she'd go to my house. Hurrying down West Fourth to Twelfth Street she saw a tall woman in front of her. At a slow trot Ilse finally overtook the woman. A fleeting look confirmed her sorrow. She wasn't Carole.

Embarrassed, she muttered, "Excuse me," and walked the rest of the way home. No one lurked in front of the building. No one was in the hallway and the courtyard was equally bare. Lucia's don't-bother-me banner hung over the balcony. Opening the door to her small cottage revealed that no one had crawled through the window. Ilse closed the door on the last vestige she had of romantic illusion and shuddered. What is it that Alice quotes or did I read it? Scratch a fascist and uncover a romantic. I wonder if it's true?

The shower lifted her a bit but her stomach was firmly tied in a knot. A dank anger pulled at her. She was mad because Carole didn't chase after her and she was even more furious at herself for secretly wishing to be chased. Slowly a sense of release untied the knot. She felt low but she felt free—not of Carole but of something, that remaining sliver of romanticism that clouds the truth and softens those hard edges of reality that should push us into action. Ilse fell asleep wondering if she was growing up in spite of herself.

The door flew open and Martin Twanger, a fat sorry looking son-of-a-bitch if ever there was one, jumped under his desk, terrified by the three furious feminists bearing down on him. Twanger, the *Village Rag's* hatchet columnist, prided himself on shocking the public. His most famous expose to date was an article "proving" over seventy-five percent of all New York City's employees had smoked marijuana, and of that number, twenty per cent admitted to oral copulation. Twanger thought he was big time. Now he looked more surprised than surprising.

"All right, Twanger, get your fat ass out from under the desk," Ilse barked.

The white walls covered with push pins, copy, and fingerprints seemed to shudder as much as New York's fearless boy reporter.

"What are you going to do," whined a high-pitched voice.

"Cut your balls off, what do you think," Alice Reardon snarled.

"You're sick," Martin managed.

"Right—of you, you hothouse phony. Now get your ass out from beneath that desk." Ilse landed a furious kick smack on his can.

"I'll sue, I'll sue." The voice was climbing into the soprano register.

"What makes you think you'll live that long?" Ilse laughed.

According to their scouting, the *Village Rag* emptied out Thursday at four. People were exhausted by copy deadlines, layouts squeaking in just on time, and the usual chaos of that weekly red-letter day when the *Rag* made it to press or else. Martin Twanger usually stayed on and the women counted on his solitary vigil with a blue pencil behind his ear for effect.

What they didn't count on was a noise behind a closed door which opened narrowly then tried to close again. Harriet, along for the fun, grabbed it and pulled it open. Hanging on the door knob was none other than Olive Holloway and a middle-aged man smoking a pipe.

"Join the party." Ilse motioned them to come in.

"Olive, what an unexpected displeasure," Alice crooned.

Olive, looking stricken, slunk out, followed by the puffing pipe. As Harriet closed the door she noticed an Emmy standing conspicuously on a cluttered desk. So that's who it is, she thought, Joshua Chernakov, who did the script for that television special on instant nostalgia: "Where is the Left?" So much for political journalism.

As color returned to Olive's face, her tongue warmed up as well. "What do you think you're doing?"

"Flushing out a rat," Harriet answered.

"Now see here, young women, I don't know what all this is about but can't you act a little more discreetly? You aren't going to really beat up Martin, are you?" Joshua spoke.

"Not with my hands, I don't want to get them dirty." Ilse glared at the pipe.

Still squeezed under his desk, Martin babbled something inaudible.

"Martin, come out from under there," Joshua commanded.

"And let these harpies tear me limb from limb? Fat chance."

"Don't come out, Martin. I know these women. They're capable of anything," Olive warned.

"Really, Olive, this is ridiculous." Joshua's voice lowered to give him a more commanding tone.

"Why don't you both shut up and sit down," Ilse ordered.

"Young lady, I don't take orders from the United States government, I won't take them from you. I was on Nixon's shit list, you know."

Ilse walked over and cracked him in the chest. Joshua Chernakov sat down with new respect in his eyes. "Well, now you're on my shit list, mister."

"See, see, I told you they're violent," Martin moaned, the desk giving his words a mystical reverberation.

"Get out from under there, Twanger," Alice softly called to him.

"I won't, I won't. You can't make me."

"Wanna bet?" Alice grabbed one chubby leg. Martin's white socks flashed like a surrender signal. "Christ, this pig really is a pig. Give me a hand."

Harriet grabbed the other, equally chubby leg, and they pulled mightily.

Martin held onto the desk legs, tears streaming down his cheeks. At this point he bordered on hysteria and said something garbled but that sounded like, "I'm too young to die, I'm too young to die."

171

Ilse, tiring of the intrepid reporter's melodrama, brought her booted foot down on his left hand with a swift crunch. As he let go, Alice and Harriet pulled as hard as they could and out he came collecting most of the floor's filth as he slid.

"Don't hurt me, don't hurt me," Martin wailed.

Neither Joshua nor Olive made a move to help the stricken man, either out of cowardice or scarcely concealed loathing for a creature both had come to depend on.

"Now sit down and shut up." Alice threw him in a seat.

"We're all going to sit here and have a polite conversation. Since Mr. Twanger needs some time to collect himself, let's start with you, Olive. You here to pick up a payoff for that rotten story you helped write about our group?"

"I don't have to answer to you."

"I'd advise it." Ilse's anger, cool, was frightening but Olive perhaps thought her female hormones would save her and missed Ilse's purpose entirely.

"Don't try to push me around, little Lenin. I'll get a lawyer as soon as I get out of here."

"You do that." Ilse backhanded her with such force Joshua's left eye began to twitch uncontrollably. "Now what are you doing here?"

With tears in her eyes, Olive whispered in a small voice, "Joshua and I were working out arrangements for me to do a monthly column on the women's movement."

"Getting smart aren't you, Olive?" Alice stared at her. "You've learned not to take things in money but in kind. I'm real impressed. How about you, Harriet?"

"Yeah, I'm real impressed." Harriet moved to get closer to Alice and she reached for Joshua's arm. Disgusted he picked her hand off his sleeve as though she were a cockroach.

"You too good for her now, Mr. Big?" Ilse sneered at him.

"I don't have anything to do with your movement battles."

"That's not quite true," Alice stated.

As he was not the center of attention, Martin Twanger made for the door. With two graceful strides Ilse was behind him and darted her right foot around his ankle. Down he went.

"Don't hurt me, don't hurt me."

"Shut up, creep."

As if walking on eggshells he made his way back to his chair.

"Martin, move over here so you can be next to your colleagues." Alice pulled up a chair next to Olive so she could enjoy his overpowering aroma.

"So you're above all this, Mr. Chernakov?"

"I didn't say that. I simply said I have nothing to do with your movement battles. You're angry at Olive for cooperating with Martin on that unfortunate article. That has nothing to do with me, really."

"Unfortunate! That was one of my best pieces," Twanger wailed.

Joshua's left eye twitched again.

"Well, Mr. Chernakov, I don't see it your way at all." Ilse started in on him. "You've made a career sucking off the male left, the Black movement, and now you're going to draw some blood from us. You just sit back in your chair while other people take all the risks and then you pass judgment on it. Yeah, I've been checking up on you. My favorite part is that then you go to cocktail parties and parade as a genuine intellectual member of the radical left. Bet the women in Valentino clothing dig it."

Chernakov sputtered, his face blotched, but Ilse, unable or unwilling to check her contempt, chopped him square in the throat and he gasped, eyes bulging. "That's a small payment for everyone you've ripped off. I wish to hell I could kill you and get away with it."

Alice put her arm through Ilse's left elbow and pulled her back gently. "Easy, Ilse, we've got work to do here."

Alice took over. "I do have to hand it to you, Chernakov, you get a flunky like Twanger to write the smear story, you hire so-called reporters to cover each of the movements, preferably everything negative they can lay their hands on, then you write the big picture piece on what's really wrong with America and the movements and your prose just sings, doesn't it? Must be quite a strain putting out an essay every two weeks. But you must get quite a nice salary for it, don't you? Just to show your heart's in the right place, wouldn't you like to contribute two thousand dollars to the rape crisis center? You could get your name on the patron's list. That'd look real good to the cocktail crowd now, wouldn't it? Show the world what a big guy you are, Joshua, you're going to take women's issues seriously, especially this issue."

Joshua's eye twitched wildly. Sweat poured over his forehead. He was a man afraid but he was afraid of something more than physical violence. "Yes, yes,

174

I'll do that." What was left of his voice after Ilse's chop cracked over every word.

"Just to make sure you won't have a change of heart, we'll check the center next Thursday to see if they've received your generous gift," Ilse added.

He nodded his head painfully. Chernakov's eyes never met theirs. He seemed to have found oneness with the floor.

Twanger yelped in disbelief, "Josh, what's wrong with you? So what if they beat us up, we'll take them to court."

Head down, Chernakov said, slowly but distinctly, "No, I think there's already been enough damage. Maybe they're right. I haven't taken any risks."

"Come on!" Twanger exploded. "What do you care what they think? You run the *Rag*, man. You can blow them out of the water. I mean this is America. We're the free press."

"This is America all right and no one is free from your kind of freedom of the press." Ilse looked at him.

Realizing he overstepped his bounds on two counts, Twanger shrank back in his chair, thoroughly dumbfounded. He was confused which frightened him more than ever.

"I get paid a lot less than Josh, you know. You're not going to hit me up for money, are you?"

"Oh, I don't know, Martin Twanger. I think you could make a small contribution to the women's press collective."

His face shriveled. "How much?"

"We'll let you off the hook for five hundred dollars." Alice nailed it home.

"Five hundred dollars?"

"Be a sport, Twanger, you spend that on grass."

"Yeah, well so does everyone else in this city."

"Did I say anything moral about it? But how would you feel if your contact went public, assuming someone muscled him and he had to, you know? New York has some strange drug laws these days and that poor guy could get salted away for years. I bet he'd be real mad at you, Martin."

"Christ, you all are like the Mafia."

"Not quite, Martin, not quite. They've got money and political power. Right now we're a little short on both counts but we're learning, we're really learning," Harriet joined in.

"Now about your contribution? Would you like to make it in your name or remain anonymous?" Ilse pressed.

"Uh, anonymous."

"One other little thing you need to do for us, Martin. You'll print a retraction of last week's slam on all counts particularly about my rich 'keeper,' " Ilse quietly requested.

Twanger's face went beet red. This hurt more than the money. Glancing at Joshua who now had his head in his hands, he thought the better of protest. "All right."

Olive, last on the list, peered apprehensively at her foes. Harriet continued on the track, "Olive, since you can't write and since you won't have access to the women's movement in the future it doesn't make much sense for you to put out a column, does it?"

"I'll do as I please, you haven't got anything on me."

Ilse started for her but Alice restrained her.

Harriet faced her down and with something approaching kindness in her voice said, "Olive, no one is going to talk to you and I doubt if Mr. Chernakov can afford to print your inner thoughts on a monthly basis."

"What do you mean, no one is going to talk to me?"

"Just that," Harriet countered.

"You don't run this movement, you can't muzzle it."

Ilse, fed up, spat at her. "It's people like you with the help of the Twangers and Chernakovs of the world that set us against one another. No one is going to talk to you, Olive. Word's out. No responsible, street-organizing feminist will give you any information or let you in her group. Sure you can talk to the other crazies like yourself but that's not news unless you want to print it in *Psychology Today*."

"You'll pay for this, Ilse—you, all of you, will pay."

"What are you going to do? Write a long piece showing how I was trained to be a C.I.A. agent while in junior high school? That's about your speed."

"Maybe I will."

"Good, Olive. You just run up the flag and see who salutes. That will save us all a lot of time in this movement discovering who's nuts and who isn't." Alice sighed, completely disgusted. "I think it's time we leave these people to their just desserts—after all it is suppertime."

"Right," Harriet replied.

As the women left the office, Olive flew off her

chair and made for the telephone. Twanger and Chernakov looked dazed.

"You two hungry?" Harriet asked.

"Why don't we go over to Mother Courage? Since word will get out fast we ought to be where people can find us, calm, you know?" Alice thought out loud.

"Oh, Alice, it's my night off. I'm there all the time."

"Discipline, Ilse. Come on, we'll buy you a pizza and you can eat it in the corner in shame and pray Dolores doesn't sniff it out. We really ought to be on solid territory and public."

"You're right, Alice. You're always right," Ilse laughed.

"You are something when you are pissed. I thought you'd kill all three of them." Harriet laughed as much out of tension as anything else.

Her anger drained her and Ilse felt nothing but exhaustion right then. "H-m-m, well, I'd have killed them if I could."

"Better not say that publicly in case any of them ever winds up dead, m'dear," cautioned Alice.

"Didn't Twanger and Olive make a pair though. Those two just go together," Harriet smirked.

"Yeah, like gin and seconal."

"Alice, you have a sharp tongue in your head. I never would have known."

"Well, usually I think it, I don't say it. Now Carole, she says it, that's why I like her."

Ilse winced.

"I'm sorry."

"So am I. What an asshole I was. I think half my fury back there at the *Village Rag* was over Carole and everything. The whole damned world!"

"Maybe you'll get back together." Harriet tried to be helpful.

"Naw, I doubt it. In ten years maybe."

"Wonder where we'll all be in ten years?" Alice asked.

"Funny, I don't have much personal sense of that. I've got ideas of where I want feminism to be in ten years, but I'm not so clear on me," Ilse replied.

"Me too," said Harriet.

"Well, I hope we're farther along than we were tonight," Ilse half laughed.

"Just think, if the Olives of the world turned all that destructive energy toward Exxon instead of other women," Alice mused.

"Maybe one thing we have to realize is that not all sisters are sisters." Harriet kicked a stone across Eleventh Street.

"Olive taught me something and I'm grateful for that," Alice said.

"What?" Ilse turned toward her.

"That sometimes you have to play rough. We can't go on acting like ladies and expect to win, you know?"

"I'm beginning to know." Ilse leaned over to see Harriet, who was on the other side of Alice.

"Don't look at me, Ilse James."

"Wasn't it you who said or borrowed from some stale poster, 'We have to replace the love of power with the power of love.' "

"Unfair, unfair. I do believe that. I guess I'm

learning how far love goes and how far it doesn't go."

"Some people learn through love and some you just have to punch in the gut." Alice now kicked the stone Harriet had sent down the road.

"Tell that to our sweet sisters."

"Sarcasm, sarcasm and cynicism from Ilse James, young fountain of feminist thought!" Harriet teased her right back.

"Laugh, go ahead and laugh but I wonder how long it will take the ostriches to pull their heads out of the sand? Everyone thinks this struggle is going to be easy, all you have to do is think good, clean thoughts, brush three times daily and chant *om* in the presence of the Great Mother. Christ, women will still be brutalized in Bolivia and Appalachia and if the President wants an undeclared war in Cambodia we may well have one. What does it take to teach women to wake up, to grow up, to stop acting like ladies!"

"Patience?" Alice offered.

"Patience, and how long do I work with patience as my reward? How much longer can any of us work for nothing? Shit, if we don't get money we could at least get a little respect. That's one thing Carole taught me, speaking of learning, that this movement operates out of the Lady Bountiful attitude and we drive out lower-class women who can't keep up because they don't have the time or the money or the babysitters."

"I'm kind of sorry Carole never came and talked to our group," Harriet mumbled.

"So am I. She's been around longer than we have. If nothing else she could give us a longer perspective."

Alice quickened her pace as her hunger set in.

"Oh, if she could hear us now. She'd wither me with, 'All this has been said before. Don't you read history?' Carole sees centuries not days." Ilse bordered on the wistful.

"No, no it hasn't all been said before. We are adding something new to consciousness. I read history. I know what in this movement is right out of 1789 and what is ours. But what scares me is that it's all talk. Do you realize that tonight for the first time we did not put out a little bulletin, we did not stage a feminist version of a craft fair, the proceeds to go to our favorite project which might as well be called a charity. Do you know what we did? We went out and fought ugly. Given those particular people nothing else would have worked but the important thing is we walked off with something. The rape crisis center will go on for three months because of tonight and the press collective will get out another mailing. We actually did something and we inspired a little fear. Seems like in America you got to prove you can hurt someone before you're taken seriously. And you want to know something else?" Alice paused, her eyes grew larger. "I liked it. I loved it. I want to win. I don't care how it sounds. I want real power. I want to say: U.S. out of Bolivia, out of Cambodia, out of people's bedrooms with your goddamned listening devices. I want to say: Pay up your fair share of taxes, U.S. Steel; build railroads instead of cars, Detroit. I want to say all that and have it stick."

Ilse put her arms around Alice's shoulders and Harriet reached up and put her arm around Alice as well. "Me, too," they both replied.

"Guess this means we don't remain pure as the driven snow," Harriet breathed out.

"Guess not. I think that 'be perfect' business that gets thrown at us all the time is really a subtle way to say 'fail.' " Ilse hopped to keep up with Alice.

At Mother Courage Alice ordered a carafe of white wine. A splurge for Alice who didn't have much money.

"A toast, sisters. Here's to growing up and discovering the world isn't a rose garden but we have to live in it anyway."

They clinked glasses and then Ilse started to laugh. "Leave it to you, Reardon, to find the right thorn at the right time."

Howling they drank another toast.

Alice, with the thoroughness characteristic of her, researched Joshua Chernakov's past and discovered he graduated from Northwestern in 1947. One of Alice's old lovers worked there as an administrator and plowed through the records as much out of curiosity as a favor to Alice. She found something a bit peculiar in Joshua's record. He was called before the Dean on unspecified charges and forced to seek outside help. The name of the doctor was not on the document but the name of the dean was. The dean, an old man, retired to Princeton, New Jersey, where he lived on the west side of town amid other relics. Alice hopped a New Jersey Transit bus out to Princeton and conned her way into the old man's presence. He recalled the case vaguely but wouldn't give out any details. Alice tried every bribe she knew—decently of course. She noticed lovely illuminated manuscripts on his wall. Desperate but determined she raced back to Carole Hanratty at N.Y.U., spilled out her plight and Ilse's intention of beating them all to a pulp if they couldn't get anything on any of the *Rag* people. Carole, full of her childhood devils, swooped into Fred's office while he was out and brazenly stole one of the department's illuminated manuscripts off the wall. Before Carole would hand over the prize she made Alice swear never to tell anyone including Ilse. Alice solemnly swore, tore out of the building, back to Port Authority, ran up to platform 122, and headed back to Princeton where she arrived in time for afternoon tea. Weakened by Alice's booty, the old fellow told his tale: Joshua Chernakov was a promising young student. His professors were quite glad he was too young to enlist or had been found unsuitable for service, no one was quite clear. A bright journalistic career loomed on Joshua's horizon. A man of social ambition, Joshua dated an icy Chicago meat-packing heiress. One weekend at a particularly rowdy college party Joshua could no longer contain his ardor. He slipped the young beauty a drugged drink and when she passed out gallantly carried her to a nearby room where he had, as grandmothers used to say, his way with her. The heiress on being driven back home, slowly awoke and, formerly a virgin, felt some pain. She also noticed a telltale stream of sperm oozing down her thigh. A brave person, considering the times, she told her parents. Horrified, they called the president of the university, told him the scandal in strictest confidence and he in turn, told the dean, whose job it is to see boys in trouble. Joshua Chernakov was in a great deal of trouble. Because he had such a good record, was so intellectually capable, the dean pleaded for him. And so a deal was struck between the meat-packer midas and the dean. Joshua could finish out his senior year but upon graduation he must leave the area and he would never work for any of the big paper chains anywhere since Midas was in tight with the publishing giants. And so Joshua Chernakov wandered to New York City and happened to be around when the *Village Rag*, a new concept in journalism, got started. He had good skills, was young and personable, could turn a neat phrase and that was the beginning of his career. No one was ever the wiser for his past. Naturally, the young woman's parents never told anyone. Rape is not a word used in polite society.

A literary calender at the left edge of Carole's desk showed the day was October fourth. Written in the square was the notation, "St. Francis of Assisi died 1226." Francis was Carole's favorite saint in her Catholic girlhood and though she left the Church she never quite turned away from this gentle man who practiced what he preached. She wrote next to the saint's name, "The Clares," the female order of Franciscans. She sat there making the capital C a darker red by retracing it absent-mindedly. Five days passed and Ilse hadn't called her and she hadn't called Ilse. She picked up the phone as though to dial the number and then dialed Adele.

"Whatcha doing?"

"Trying to teach Lester 'The Charge of the Light Brigade.' "

"How's he doing?"

"So far he's a whizz at 'Into the valley of death

184

rode the squawch.' "

"Would it disturb his study if I came over for tea?"

"No, might be good for him. All this blood, guts, and gore is straining the little fellow. I'll make a pot of Twinings English Breakfast or would you like Russian Caravan?"

"Uh, Russian Caravan, a good flavor for the late morning, don't you think?"

"Hurry up, it'll be brewed by the time you get here."

Indian summer warmed the sidewalks. Briskly Carole walked to Adele's. Window boxes offered up their last crop of the year, late blooming roses, marigolds, and sturdy zinnias. A twinge of regret for summer tugged at her although fall was the most exciting season. The beginning of the academic semester filled her with new students and new ideas. Friends came back from abroad or wherever and the city's pulse quickened. The only trouble with fall was that she knew winter followed. A bakery shop's smells enticed her to buy croissants and fresh butter.

When Carole rang the bell Adele, in her eagerness to see her friend, forgot to close the door to the bird cage which she had been cleaning. She ran over to unlock the front door. Lester unfurled his crown and craned his neck to see if this was too good to be true.

"Pot's ready." Adele gave Carole a big bear hug as she walked in the door. "What's in there?"

"Goodies. What's Lester doing flying through the living room, Adele?"

"Lester!"

Mad with power and being the center of attention,

Lester bellowed, "Bwana, White Devil, Bwana. Ack, Ack."

The other birds squealed and clicked their tongues. Adele raced for the cage and closed the door before the other creatures got big ideas.

Carole laughed. "Sounds like a goddamned Dolores Del Rio movie."

"Maybe if we advance slowly he'll retreat and I can back him into the cage. You hold the door ready."

"We can't back him up. He's flying over our heads. Maybe you should try the broom."

"Good idea, then I can break his little neck." At the sight of the broom waving in the air Lester became bolder. "Not the sofa, Lester, not the sofa." Naturally he passed over the sofa and shat with amazing accuracy. "LaVerne is going to kill me."

"I feel like Doolittle bombing Tokyo."

"No, dear, you feel like the Japanese. Lester's doing all the bombing around here." Adele put her hands on her hips.

"Let's try another approach," Carole suggested. She raised her voice and smiled. "Lester, pretty Lester. Come on, birdie, come on, time to go back to your nice home."

"Balls said the queen. Ack, ack."

"Whoever said 'birdbrain' is a derogatory term didn't know much about birds." Adele by this time was laughing at Lester's outrageous behavior which only made him do it more.

"If I had two I'd be king. Bwana, White Devil."

"Racist."

Lester headed for the feathered flag on the wall. He attacked it vigorously which made Adele scream at the top of her lungs. Carole threw her hands over her head like a referee signaling the kick is wide. She rushed him. He gained altitude and circled coming back at the flag with his feet this time.

"Lester, anything, just leave my flag alone," Adele moaned.

Secure in his victory he got fresh and zoomed close to Adele's head, the brightly colored feathered bits in his talons brushing her nose. He circled again, nearly hit the ceiling and made for Carole. It was all systems go. Lester was having the time of his life.

"I may kill that bird before LaVerne gets the chance," Carole threatened, brushing off her sleeve.

"We're both so damn dumb. I know what'll get him. You stay here and keep him occupied while I sneak into the kitchen."

"Keep him occupied. I'll be a target."

"The price of eternal friendship."

"What are you getting in the kitchen?"

"Potato chips."

Lester heard her crinkling the bag and rested on the chair. He screwed his head around until it was close to upside down. Hopping from foot to foot he opened his mouth and croaked. He threw his head back and chattered a whole row.

"Look what Mommy has, you home wrecker. Lookie, lookie." She held up a large potato chip and continued to crinkle the bag with her other hand. "Now if you want this delicious Wise's potato chip you're going into your cage."

Slowly Adele moved toward the cage. The temptation of that huge, golden potato chip was too much. Lester followed. Adele sprinkled a shower of chips in the cage and Lester, tired from all his flying, waddled in the cage like a tiny Jemima Puddleduck. Triumphant, Adele slammed the cage. "Gotcha!"

Carole went over to the cage and put her arm around Adele's shoulder. The two of them shook with laughter. Lester devoured the chips, looking at them from time to time. The turtle down in the water stuck her head out to get a better view and to steal a chip. She got one before Lester could stop her. Lester would never mess with the turtle. The mynah let out a wolf whistle and Lester muttered, "Piss."

"Hey, bird, Momma's gonna cram bee-bees down your gullet so you can't fly," Adele purred. "Devil."

"That's his line."

"Now that the commotion has died down let me bring a knife and two small plates so we can eat ourselves."

"Can I do anything?"

"No, you've already suffered enough. Speaking of suffering, has Ilse called since the fight?"

"No and I haven't called her either." Carole buttered the buns while Adele fussed over the tea in the kitchen.

"Too bad you didn't stop by a Chinese bakery. You could have bought fortune cookies and all our guessing would be over."

"With my luck the little white strips would be mottos written by Mary Baker Eddy."

"You don't look devastated although you sound a touch sarcastic, my dear."

"You know me, Dell. My only regret is that I never dipped Ilse's breasts in champagne. How could I? Beer might have met her qualifications but it's hardly the same."

Adele laughed. "Someone ought to tell that child the reason for revolution is so the good things in life circulate."

"Oh, well."

"Why don't you call her?"

"No, we're both too raw. It wouldn't do any good. Maybe I'll write her a short note. I don't know. Can't make up my mind."

"Mmm."

"I never did put much faith in love relationships. I mean it always seemed to me that an element of lying is necessary to keep them going."

"Probably, for most people. Games and all. There's nothing wrong with not wanting that. It's just that the world we live in is in couples whether they're straight or whether they're gay. The world goes by twos."

"The idea of having someone say my name linked with someone else's never did sit well with me. Noah would have left me off the ark."

"Honey, he'd have left us all off the ark." Adele's eyes twinkled.

"God knows."

"Look at it this way. Now you won't have to spend your time sparring and you won't have to look at those messy women you used to complain about."

"I guess I did."

"Can't say as I blame you."

"The first time I saw that crew it was like someone hit me in the face with a wet fish. I'll never understand why a woman would want to make herself purposefully ugly. Ilse said men made us sex objects and those women reacted against that. But there must be come middle ground between Godzilla and Miss America?"

"Queen Kong?"

"There's a thought."

"The time we were in Mother Courage and a few of them straggled in . . ." Adele paused.

"Yes?"

"What struck me was their appearance, of course, but I sat there and thought to myself—now that is truly stupid. By making themselves as ugly as . . . "

"Homemade dogshit."

"Carole!"

"You forget, we said it too down in Richmond."

"Where was I? Oh, by making themselves so unattractive they are still allowing themselves to be defined by men. A negative reaction is just as limiting as a positive one. If they really had themselves together they'd do whatever made them feel good, the hell with men one way or the other. I always dress for myself and we all know how Miss Adele loves flashy threads."

"And you look terrific. You're right, I never thought of appearance that way—definition. I just figured they were walking around with a fatal dose of self hate."

"Same difference, maybe."

"Maybe."

"I am so glad to see you're not way down. I know you liked that girl."

"Woman."

"Oh hell, she's a girl to me. She's twenty-two years younger than I am."

190

"Can't say as I've figured out the line between girl-hood and womanhood myself. I did like her. I do like her. Ah! the tea cup is hot." Carole put the cup back down.

"Sorry, I should've warned you those extra big cups keep the heat."

"All this did bring a few threads together for me. Things I overlooked or ignored."

"Oh?"

"Adele, this may sound crazy but I'm longing for my childhood. Remember that time when things were pure?"

"Yes, yes, I know what you mean."

"I've lost some of me and I want it back. An idea keeps going around in my head to go back to my roots. Don't look surprised. I want to go back to Richmond or outside Winchester where Grams had the farm. I don't know how or when. There are universities and colleges around. I ought to be able to get some kind of job."

"Leave the city?"

"I love the city even when it's awful but it's not my home. I want to go home. I want roots."

"But, Carole, you've got roots here, all your friends."

"I know, I know, but it's not the same. I know this sounds silly but somehow it's hitting me that I want to go back where I came from. Not in time and not back to the slums but back to the area, the land."

"If ever there was a Southern philosophy, that's it. The land. I can't say that I haven't felt that way myself. I don't exactly long for the folk's mansion in St. Louis but I wonder sometimes if I haven't run away and called it opportunity? I often wonder should I go teach at a small Black college if they can make room for me. It does run through my head. I don't do anything about it because of Verne. Her chance is right here. Maybe in time she'll want to go and then we'll do it. But until that time, if it ever comes, I'll stay here unless I get the call."

"I think I've got the call. I'm going—I just don't know when or where. Richmond, Winchester, University of Virginia?"

"It's not the whole answer. It isn't like you're an urban vagabond. We do have some community here."

"I know, Adele, I do know. But what impact can we have on this city? Our jobs give us some chance to do something but it's not enough any more. I'm tired of professionalism in that narrow sense. I want more. I want to go somewhere where my voice isn't so small. Back to my roots. Maybe that's part of what's wrong with America. We've been running away from our roots since World War I and now we're all lost. Opportunity turned out to be not enough. Job status isn't the same thing as being valued in your community. Do you know what I mean?"

"I feel the frustration, I know, but I figure the city is the women's frontier. Besides, who's going to listen to a lesbian? At least here you can be open to an extent."

"Well, if we all keep hiding in the giant cities we're cheating ourselves . . . but the women's movement *has* made a difference. There's more room now. I'm not saying it's easy but maybe that's just what we have to do, Adele, go back where we came from and fight this out."

192

"Carole?"

"No, I haven't turned into a revolutionary, not yet anyway. But I'm beginning to see there's more to my life than just me. And part of what can help me find some peace—going back home—may turn out to help women there—and men too if they care to learn."

"If that doesn't give you inner peace then you've got nothing left but evangelism and brandy," joked Adele.

"Or worse, I'll be condemned to reflection."

"Before you sentence yourself let me bring some chocolate chip cookies. We can dip them in our tea."

"If we'd bought stock in coca cola and nabisco when we started teaching we'd be rich by now."

Adele sailed back in with the cookies on a plate. "Carole, I can't imagine being without you." Her voice was soft. "I know you wouldn't go for at least a year or two but we've been together all these years. It doesn't seem possible."

"I . . . whenever I start thinking about my roots I remind myself that you're part of those roots, the best part."

"Thank you."

"Maybe by the time I'm ready you two will feel like moving."

"Verne and I never really talked about it but I'll bring it up. She might surprise both of us. Bloomies isn't the center of the earth. Maybe she'll set off in a spirit of enterprise and start her own little store or something. If we're near colleges there will be a market for clothes and the clever things she picks up."

"Ask her. You know she might see it as an adventure. And there's no reason we couldn't all move back to New York if things didn't work out." She paused. "Adele, have you ever wondered why we never became lovers?"

"Now there's a bolt out of the blue. What brought that on?"

"This last fling and thoughts of moving. It suddenly became clear to me I love you more than anyone on earth."

"Dammit." Adele spilled her tea.

"Stay there and I'll get a paper towel." Carole came back from the kitchen and mopped up the tea. "Clutz."

"No. Surprised."

"I've thought of it thousands of times—I mean that you're dear to me. I guess I never thought it had to be said. Where I come from you don't have to say things like that, people know."

"I know, I knew, I . . . it's fine. God, I sound like I'm conjugating."

Carole laughed. *"Amo, amas, amat."*

*"Amamus, amantis, amant.* Did I get it right?"

"How the hell do I know? I just read the stuff, I never hear it."

"While we're at this, I want a turn. Why do you think we never went to bed?"

"You never asked me."

"Carole Hanratty, that's obscene. Me ask you?"

"What did you think? I was going to ask you?"

"Jesus christ."

"What's he got to do with this?"

"I figured you weren't turned on by Black women."

"Adele, are you serious?"

"Of course I'm serious. Would I say a dumb thing

194

like that if I didn't mean it?"

"Well, when we met it was volatile. But once we became friends that sort of thing faded. In fact, color became rather silly. How could anyone take it seriously?"

"Yeah, I know, but the only way we found out was to spend time together. Ilse's generation has a better chance on that than we did. I always thought you were beautiful, spectacular. You know that?"

"No, I knew you liked me but . . . "

"You're still beautiful, Carole, inside and out."

"You too, Dell. When you walk into the room I smile. Even when I'm depressed as hell your presence makes me smile. Makes me glad I'm breathing. I don't know, somehow we missed our sexual connection. When I met you, you were going with whoozits. By the time I was attempting my forever relationship, well, that was just the time you broke up. Then, boom, you met LaVerne. So now how will we ever make love?"

"Ha."

"We can't sneak around on LaVerne. I adore her. I couldn't do anything like that neither could you. Dell, we screwed up."

"Oh, we're not dead yet. Anyway, maybe that's one of the reasons we're so tight, the possibility of making love was always there underneath. We never acted on it. Maybe we will. Maybe we won't but if we don't it won't be tragic. I have to say I don't know if I could handle it. I've always been, what's that awful word, monogamous?"

"We'd be almost incestuous, wouldn't we?"

"Sisters?"

"Sisters." Carole leaned over and kissed Adele on the cheek. "You know what else I've been thinking?"

"My dear, at this point I couldn't possibly imagine."

"Ilse did show me some things. I was thinking I ought to write a book about outstanding women in the Middle Ages. Not much has been done about women back then."

"Back then? Any time."

"You take the Mayan women and I'll take European women in the Middle Ages. With my background it wouldn't be too difficult to put together a book of heroines, women like Eleanor de Montfort in the thirteenth century and Queen Margaret who won the battle of St. Albans. There's so much material that ought to be brought to light. That's not the same as organizing a child care center but it's something I can do. And I think it's important to know what our ancestors did."

"I think it's a glorious idea. You know I think all the dead are our ancestors. We should pay attention to them."

"I was hoping you'd say that."

"It's a beautiful day. Come on, let's walk in the park. Want to?"

"Sure."

As they walked out the front door into the early afternoon sun, Adele turned to Carole. "You know what I think?"

"My dear, I couldn't begin to guess."

"I think the secret of life is there is no secret." Adele threw her hand to the sun with a flourish.

"I think you're right."